GW00771913

About the author

Nicholas Faulkner is a chartered surveyor and has lived in rural Hampshire for the last 25 years. He occasionally lectures on property law and acts as an expert witness.

He is married to Gloria and spends his spare time gardening, travelling with his family and keeping up with current affairs.

Writing fiction has become a source of relaxation and enjoyment and an outlet for a creative side which he hasn't exercised for many years. He is currently writing his third novel.

A Dream to Die For

Published in 2014 by Splendid Media Group (UK) Limited

Splendid Media Group (UK) Limited
The Old Hambledon Racecourse Centre
Sheardley Lane
Droxford
Hampshire
SO32 3QY
United Kingdom

www.splendidmedia.co.uk
info@splendidmedia.co.uk

British Library Cataloguing in Publication Data is available from The British Library

978-1-909109-31-5

Commissioning Editor: Steve Clark

Designed by Swerve Creative • www.swerve-creative.co.uk

Printed in the UK

A Dream to Die For

Nicholas Faulkner

For Gloria, Gabriel and Giorgia

Acknowledgements

The writing of this book has been rewarding and relaxing simultaneously! However to bring this to publication has not been without the assistance and support of a number of people. Principally my wife Gloria and children Gabriel and Giorgia have had to suffer as husband and father tried to pretend he had some creative talent beyond the day job. When it came to that day job, my team in the Portsmouth office have had to listen to a variety of drafts over lunch hours for months and their continued support has been great. Particular mention should go to Sarah Metherell who contributed the idea for the title. Finally my thanks to Steve Clark who, as well as being one of my oldest friends, has piloted me through the publication process with a balance of patience and tenacity.

PROLOGUE

MIKE opened his eyes to a bright light. His head felt as though he had the hangover from hell. His mouth was dry and his throat hurt. His head pounded so badly he did not want to lift it from the pillow, yet he needed to look around as he was unsure where he was.

'Would you like a sip of water?' A calm smiling face was by his side, a nurse, so, he concluded, he must be in hospital.

'Thanks, God my head hurts,' Mike replied. He watched the nurse lean down and move a lever so the back of his bed started to raise gently. As it did so, the little hospital room where he was lying started to come into view. He was alone in the room, which had space for his bed, a chair to the side under the window and then various monitors on stands either side of the headboard. Each one appeared to be connected to him through tubes and wires. Screens showed continuous graphs of thin lines running across from left to right. His left arm had a drip line attached to a clear plastic bag which stood on a stand just beside one of the monitors. A small side table to his right contained a vase with flowers, a book and two Get Well Soon cards.

After the bed stopped moving the nurse passed him a small glass of water that she had poured from a plastic jug. It had been placed on a table that seemed to cover the bottom part of the bed and hide the lower part of his body.

'I know you are very thirsty, but please try and just sip this a little at a time. You may feel nauseous, in which case I have a bowl just here.' The nurse stood to the side of the bed and Mike thought she looked rather concerned.

'Please don't worry, I am sure I will be fine. I am just so thirsty.' Mike took the glass and started to drink. He quickly passed the glass back to the nurse as he started to retch. The nurse gently held his head with her right hand and Mike was sick into the waiting bowl that she held in her other.

'Oh God, I am so sorry,' said Mike as he looked up from the bowl and the splatters of vomit that were across his bedclothes. His mouth now tasted even worse than it had done so before.

'I'll go and fetch something to get you cleaned up and then the doctor will want to examine you.' The nurse continued in a calm voice. 'I think your parents are in the canteen, they are probably grabbing something to eat – they have been here all the time. I shall let them know you have woken up.' The nurse turned and left through the open door to the corridor. Mike noticed she shut the door as she left the room.

Mike sat back on his pillow, propped up in his bed, and looked again around the room. The pain in his head was eclipsed by the taste of vomit in his mouth. He had time to think.

He remembered graduating and collecting his scroll in the great hall. He had liked swanning around for most of the day in his gown and mortar-board hat, but what had happened next?

He remembered a meal, yes a long table in that nice Italian restaurant by the river, his parents were there, and there had been a lot of noise, laughing… he could not remember who else had been at the table, but he did remember the feeling of happiness.

Mike's mother opened the door of the room and walked in. Behind her was his father and then a doctor with a bow tie and a white coat, a stethoscope hung around his neck like a scarf.

'Oh darling, you must feel dreadful,' his mother uttered, as she came straight across to the bed and hugged him, tears almost instantly cascading down her face. She straightened up and as she did so the nurse came back with an even larger bowl and a flannel and towel folded across her arm.

'Mrs Stapleford, if you could let the nurse just clean up young Mike and I can have a quick look at him.' The doctor removed his stethoscope from the back of his neck and clipped the ends into his ear. He held Mike's wrist, looked at his watch and then listened to his heart, all as the nurse cleaned up the vomit and gave his face a wash with a warm damp flannel.

All the time Mike's father stood at the bottom of the bed, not saying anything. Mike could see the tears running down his cheeks and his shoulders shuddering as he tried to keep his emotions in check. At last the doctor had finished and, after another small sip of water that Mike managed to keep down, the nurse left the room, closing the door behind her.

'Can someone tell me what the hell happened and for that matter when?' Mike could not contain himself any longer, his head was starting to clear and he felt as though everyone was in on the secret but him.

'What do you last remember?' the doctor asked.

'The graduation ceremony and it gets kind of hazy but a meal at the Italian by the river. You guys were there,' Mike nodded his head towards his parents, 'but I can't really remember anyone else, except I know we were in a big party, we were celebrating.' Mike felt a little uncomfortable, he didn't like not being able to remember.

'We were celebrating after the graduation, darling, your dad and I are so proud of you, a law graduate. All your friends were at the restaurant: James, Ed, Stuart, that lovely girl Frances… well there were loads of us. And after the meal you went off to have fun and your father and I went back to our hotel. That was last Friday, I am afraid it's now Wednesday. We have been so worried about you.' Mike's mother burst into tears again and his father moved a comforting arm around her shoulders.

'We don't really know what happened,' said the doctor. 'You were found in a street. From your injuries, you were clearly knocked down by a car.'

'Well I guess that explains why I feel so bloody awful!' Mike replied. 'Although I'm shocked to have lost four days or so, have I been unconscious all that time?'

'Pretty much,' said the doctor. 'We have been keeping you sedated, as we had to perform some major operations. I am sorry to have to tell you, Mike, but I am afraid your legs were one hell of a mess when they brought you in.'

Mike realised that he had not yet moved his lower body.

'What do you mean? How much of a mess?' Mike's voice quivered, he wanted to keep it together, but seeing his parents crying again did not help.

The doctor sat down on the side of the bed and took Mike's hand.

'Look Mike, it's like this. We saved both your legs, but you will find it almost impossible to walk again unaided. The bone damage is such that they will not support your weight as they used to. After some physio, you'll be fine to walk short distances, but we're going to spend a lot of time with you…'

the doctor paused '…getting you used to a wheelchair.'

'Nooooooo!' Mike screamed as loud as he had ever done in his life.

CHAPTER 1

HE HAD not even attended her funeral.

It was his first thought as he woke.

He turned to pick up his watch from his bedside table, it was luminous and the silent dials told him it was 2.45 in the morning. He got up and walked rather unsteadily to the en-suite for a pee. His trip being a succession of lurches from one piece of furniture to another. Ever since he had been a small boy whenever he woke during the night he took the opportunity of going to the toilet, a habit he could not change, even if he wanted to.

The crescent moon was bright through the window, shining across the fields and silhouetting the tree line. He climbed back into bed and curled around his wife. She was fast asleep, unaware of his disturbed slumber, his dream, his conversation with the dead.

For the next hour, Mike replayed the dream in his head. He had been sitting in a room, talking with Andrea.

'I know you're dead,' he had said. It sounded accusing but he had not meant it to be.

'Yes I am, but that doesn't stop us from chatting. It's rather strange here, although to be honest I am not really sure where here is.' Her voice was the same as he had remembered: light, clear, soft but not too girlie.

She looked the same, her blonde hair just flowing over her shoulder, those amazing piercing blue eyes. She was in a grey dress that ended just below the knee, and black boots. The dress curved around her hips and breasts but did not hug her figure. She looked smart, professional, business-like in fact.

'It is amazing to see you, to talk to you, I miss you.' Mike had often thought of Andrea since last October, when he'd received news of the accident.

'I wanted to get in touch, but I couldn't work out how to do it,' she replied. 'There isn't a manual here to look things up.' She laughed at her own joke. 'I suppose it is a little like living, you're not given a manual there either and you work things out or ask others.'

'Is there anybody to ask?' Mike was intrigued, he wanted to find out more, but did not want to appear pushy.

'Not really.'

This was not the reply Mike had been hoping to hear. He was sat opposite Andrea to the side of a table, his arm leaning casually on it. It felt as though they were sitting in a sort of kitchen, although there wasn't the usual cooker, fridge, cabinets or anything else in sight. In fact Mike couldn't tell what was in the room except the chair he was sitting on, the table and the chair that Andrea was sitting on.

She was about five feet away from him. Sitting cross-legged, looking smart, chatting… but she was dead.

'It's not as though it's lonely here. You see people and everyone seems friendly, as though you are sort of distant acquaintances or you met them at some work function and cannot quite remember their name!'

'Have you met anyone you knew before?' Mike asked the question before he had really thought about it. He had no idea if her parents were alive or dead or if she had lost any other close relatives. How insensitive could he get! Still, too late now, the question had been asked. He wondered if he could offend someone who was already dead.

'No not yet, and in fact I don't know if I was expecting to.' Andrea had not seemed to notice Mike's thoughtless question. 'When I say you see people it is not in the same way. You don't see with your eyes, you sort of sense them being around and it's comforting.'

'That sounds rather difficult to understand. I guess you have to be there, wherever there is!' Mike liked talking to Andrea, yet he could not quite get his head around the fact that he was talking to someone who was dead.

'Well, however it works here, all I can tell you is I wanted to contact you and I am pleased I did. What I'm not certain is how long I can stay. I think I should be getting going soon.' Andrea stood and went to move out of the room. Only there was no door to open, the wall just seemed to melt away.

Mike followed and they were walking through grass. It wasn't exactly a field, it was cut and felt tended. Mike was unaware what he was wearing; he just kept following Andrea as she walked purposefully in a diagonal direction past blocks of white. The blocks seemed to be like caravans, only they had no windows. It did not seem cold or wet or windy yet they were outside. It was daylight but not bright sunshine. Mike was intrigued, was this the afterlife? It seemed rather grey and dull, not quite what he had hoped for when he had made those all too infrequent visits to his local church and had prayed to heaven.

After a few hundred yards, Andrea turned and looked at Mike.

'I am off now. It would be nice to see you again for a catch up. Shall we say the same place?'

With that Andrea just vanished. Mike stared at the space where she had stood. How could he remember where to come back to? Was it here by the hawthorn hedge that they were meant to meet again?

'When?' Mike shouted after Andrea. Even if he could find the place, a time and date would have been useful! Somehow he thought he would need to write it in his Filofax. Although Mike tried hard to keep up with modern technology, he still trusted his handwritten diary and contacts pages.

Mike snuggled his nose against the back of his wife's neck, he must have been thinking about that dream now for over an hour. How silly, he could not have been talking to the dead. He stretched his arm over his wife's body and pulled her close. She made a slight sound – an acknowledgement of pleasure – while not actually waking up. He felt the warmth of her body beneath one of his T-shirts that she always borrowed to sleep in. He felt safe.

He always felt safe as he held Victoria in bed. He had been married now for almost twenty years. Whenever something was out of the ordinary, he felt safe when he held his wife as she slumbered.

There was no doubt as to why he hadn't attended Andrea's funeral after the accident. So many of his colleagues had been there. And, despite the fact that her family had been rather distant, they had attended and he would have felt far too uncomfortable to be there.

What would they all have said if they had seen him convulse in agony as he had seen the open coffin with her body inside. Would people have put two and two together and realised that they had been so much more than colleagues? They had shared those long lunches over the last year or more, those snatched moments in the office kitchen as they made coffee and pretty well everything in between except a bed for the night.

As much as Mike had tried to reconcile the situation since Andrea's death, there was no doubt in his soul that they had been having an affair, even if they had not consummated the relationship.

'For fuck's sake, how close did he have to be!' He thought to himself as he wrapped his wife up in his arms. Yes he had felt so much more for Andrea than he had done for anyone else in years… but she was dead!

Victoria was here, now! She was his wife, he could smell her, taste her and feel her. And yet he knew she was not and never would be the Andrea that had never left his thoughts since that ghastly day last autumn when he had received the news.

Reading that email about her sudden death had simply knocked the stuffing out of him. Just two days earlier he had found an excuse to 'have a word' and, as he waited near her desk for her to finish the telephone call, he had spent the time watching her, her dazzling eyes, her long blonde hair as it cascaded over her shoulders, the curves of her breasts in that lovely silk dress. He was captivated by Andrea and had been for the last four years since she had joined the practice.

At first he had worried if his contact with her had caused any sort of notice from his peers, but apparently it had not. No one had assumed that anything had ever gone on. And so he and Andrea had grown fond of each other. The lunches had grown in length and frequency. He had enjoyed their texts in the morning as they travelled on their respective trains into London.

The funeral however had presented an entirely different level of problem. Surely everyone would notice Mike's grief – it would be better if he stayed away. Better for him no doubt, but not better for his soul that craved the chance to say its goodbye. In the end, he had decided to spend the hour or so of the funeral sitting quietly at the back of St Paul's Cathedral, thinking of his lovely Andrea and how they could no longer be together. He had sobbed to himself and only just managed to pull himself together as a lone attendant had come and stood quietly behind him, placing a comforting hand on his shoulder.

Like many decisions in Mike's life, he had learned to live with it, or so he thought. He had learnt to live firstly with the guilt of the relationship, then the loss and finally the grief at not being able to say goodbye. Most of all, he had learnt to hide his feelings for such a wonderful woman deep inside him so no one but he knew of their love.

And so what the hell was that dream all about, out of nowhere?

The alarm came from out of the blue, heralding another Wednesday. As usual Victoria stretched across from under the duvet to press the snooze button for another ten minutes.

Mike rolled over on to his side to cuddle his wife.

'Love you, gorgeous,' he said as he put an arm over her body and they settled down for those last few precious minutes before they would have to start their daily routines.

'You seemed to have a bit of a disturbed night, darling,' she said, as she sleepily relaxed in his embrace.

He thought about saying, 'Yes, sorry about that, I was having a conversation with my dead friend!' but Mike knew he could not say a word. He did not want to keep a secret from Victoria, but he also realised the more he told her the more questions there would be about his relationship with Andrea.

He knew it had been a dream, but somehow he had felt he had really had a conversation with his dead friend. That conversation had been personal, somehow Mike felt he had a need to keep it private, it was his and he didn't want to he share it. His dream was just an extension of his relationship with Andrea.

Even the whole idea was so far off the scale as to have him worry about his own sanity… conversing with the dead indeed!

'You know darling, just too much on at work and I'm feeling it is all getting on top of me,' Mike lied. He instantly felt terrible. He hated himself for not sharing with his wife. After he had lost Andrea he had tried hard to rekindle what relationship Victoria and he had had. He had never actually slept with anyone else, he told himself. Holding hands hardly constitutes adultery in court! But somehow the dream had thrust him back into a time of deception and now seemed an extension of his relationship with Andrea.

The alarm went again – their ten minute treat of a lie-in was over.

'Will you do the cats before you leave? And any chance of the rubbish?' Victoria asked as she threw the duvet off with an air of one who is resigned that the day has arrived and would need to be met head on, even if she didn't feel at that moment equipped to cope.

'Sure, no probs. I am on the later train, thank God it is the 7.06. I'm starting to hate the 6.26.' Mike moved his tired limbs to the edge of the bed to swing his legs out into the waiting wheelchair. Somehow in bed he could move around just as anybody else could, or at least that's what he thought. It was hard for him to remember now what it had been like to walk normally. His accident at 21 was such a distant memory, he had spent now more of his life getting around in a wheelchair than he had walking.

Somehow he always still managed to walk in his dreams. He stood, occasionally he ran, and yes, he always walked. His disability had not altered his life much. He could walk with the aid of two sticks, stand and manoeuvre himself in and out of his chair remarkably quickly. When it came to driving himself he could always open the boot, pack the wheelchair up and then walk around to the car door with his two sticks, get in and drive himself off. The wheelchair gave him speed and an ability to carry his case and laptop without the risk of falling over if he tried to move too fast for a commuter train.

After his shower and shave, Mike dressed in his customary blue suit and pink shirt and tie and slipped on his black oxford shoes, leaning over in his wheelchair to tie them up.

God, he must get round to polishing his shoes this weekend, they looked scruffy. He would have been given a detention at school if he had turned up with shoes in that condition, but after all these years that was one school habit that had been lost.

Mike pushed himself down the corridor and through the kitchen to the utility room where the cats were eagerly waiting for the back door to be opened and their food to be placed outside for breakfast.

That done, Mike pushed himself back into the kitchen where he collected the bin bags from under the sink and made his way back through the utility room, out of the same back door and down the ramp to deposit the bags in the two bins.

General waste black and recycling brown, Mike said to himself as he lifted the lids. He looked up at the sky and the crescent moon was still there, moved of course through the night but it was the same moon that had greeted him at quarter to three that morning just after he had met Andrea again.

'I'm off darling,' Mike shouted from the front door as he turned the key in the lock.

‘Well you could at least give me a kiss goodbye!’ Victoria called from their bedroom. She had just finished making the bed and was moving into the en-suite to shower.

‘Of course!’ Mike pushed himself down the corridor. In a way, he did adore his wife, but did he feel blessed that she was in his life? Well, perhaps he had been getting back to that point before his dream.

‘Love you,’ he said as he kissed her tenderly on the lips. She had bent down and snuggled his neck

‘Early night, I think this evening,’ she whispered in his ear. She straightened up and turned to the basin to start her morning routine of eye cream, teeth, shower and then moisturising, always in the same order.

Mike always liked those whispers in his ear. Not because they always meant instant gratification in a way that if they were ever heard by a third party they may be so portrayed, but more because they represented a closeness and companionship that Mike was once again learning to appreciate. It was not always about sex, although when that occurred, Mike was as grateful as any husband after twenty or so years.

Mike pushed himself to the car and, after the short drive to the station, he was on the platform, cappuccino in hand, waiting for the 7.06 to Waterloo.

Despite commuting into London from Winchester for the best part of a decade, Mike knew few people on the platform by name. He nodded a greeting to a couple of faces he recognised and got ready to stand up and get on the train on his sticks. The guard was on hand as usual to fold his chair up and pop it on the train at the end of the carriage where he climbed into a seat.

After finishing his coffee he closed his eyes. He often dozed off on the train, but on this morning he wondered if he would be able to recreate his dream and speak with Andrea.

CHAPTER 2

IT WAS another hard but uneventful week at work for Mike. He had commuted into London to the solicitor's practice where he was a partner every day for most of the last two decades, the last eight of which from Winchester. He found it easier to endure during the summer months and perhaps he was feeling his age in the cold January. Usually he tried to either have one day out in his car visiting clients or working from home, but that week he had not been able to arrange his diary for either.

As the end of January approached and the frosty starts each day continued, Mike worried about February. February should have meant a gradual improvement in the weather and a thought of spring around the corner. Mike often struggled with the dark winter months and the idea of cheerful daffodils heralding the start of spring should have cheered up the heart. However, for Mike he first had to address the annual stress of Valentine's Day. For most men who had been married, happily or not, for around twenty years, the day held some dread. Would flowers be enough? Would chocolates be viewed as a kick in the teeth by the unthinking husband who was not supporting his wife on the way towards those precious few pounds lost at Weight Watchers each week? Or what of the risk of that black lacy underwear purchase, sexy but not slutty? The sort of buy that most middle-aged men like Mike wanted to risk because, if received in the right spirit by the other half, led towards that lovely rekindling of passion.

What a risk though, get it wrong and the gates of hell would break loose: 'What do you think I am, some sort of slutty secretary? I'm your fucking wife, in case you had forgotten!' Mike ran through the possibilities and the possible outcomes.

'What would I have purchased for Andrea?' He mused to himself one day as he slumbered on the train home. Probably a quiet lunch, a small bistro he knew around the corner from Carnaby Street, and some flowers, traditional but discreet, not too ostentatious. Only there would be no such lunch, she was dead.

Mike turned his thoughts to Victoria. He really must try harder to connect with his wife. However for Valentine's Day Mike faced one particular problem that most men did not…

Victoria was a florist.

She had owned her own shop now for nearly five years. It was in a side street in Winchester and, although not a natural entrepreneur, she was enthusiastic in running her business but tended to panic when things did not go smoothly. The first two weeks of February brought that annual pressure. With their considerable range of friends locally, VF's, as the shop Victoria's Flowers was affectionately referred to by the regular clientele, was inundated.

Mike found the first two weeks in February almost unbearable. It was the same questions, the same lack of confidence, the same inability to make a decision, the same impact upon their smooth well-ordered lives. Or so he thought.

'Why do I do this? It cannot be worth this level of aggravation?' Victoria began the annual rant on time as if responding to a pistol at the start of a running race. She had been in the blocks, under starters orders and taut with anticipation of the adrenaline rush that was about to engulf her… it was the 5th February.

'Should I get in extra staff? I could see if Sophie has some spare time from university, Jules said she was likely to be back home studying for a couple of weeks.' Jules was Victoria's best friend, confident and an all-round pain in the arse as far as Mike was concerned. Sophie was her daughter and usually away at university where she was studying law. Mike was like most middle-aged men, acutely aware that he should not lust after 19-year-old blonde-haired students who played netball for their university, but somehow he could not help himself. He did not hate himself for his lustful thoughts about Sophie, but rather tried to accept them as some sort of primeval instinct that he could not control. He may not have altogether understood them, but inevitably had to accept them as nature, while knowing he should keep them under control. Caged tiger sounded a little too primeval for Mike's tastes but it kind of summed it up.

'For God's sake,' he thought as he allowed his mind to wander to Sophie, 'Victoria is always banging on about Tom Cruise in that bloody awful film.'

'Well, give her a call sweetie,' he said aloud. It was hard for Mike not to sound irritable, it did seem a pretty logical step and one that had been followed for the last two years, so he wondered why his views over such a simple decision were being sought.

'Should I order more red roses? Or will people want a variety of flowers such as red tulips?' Victoria asked.

The questions were now going to come thick and fast and with the monotony of a goods train, lumbering towards its final destination: the inevitable row at platform 1!

'Well how many did you order in last year, darling?' Mike tried to keep his voice calm and helpful.

'You have that managing me voice on,' Victoria retorted. 'Your know how this time of year stresses me out, you know I value your input and yet you patronise me with that tone. You are meant to love and support me you know… or did that slip your mind as you were away in your head. What were you thinking about anyway, because it sure as hell was not me!'

'Bloody hell that goods train is gathering speed faster than most years,' thought Mike.

'Well actually I was thinking about Sophie's long legs and how she looks great bending over the flower buckets on the floor of your shop!' Was what he was so tempted to say. Or was he? His head was often filled with so many different thoughts. Yes, of course, the fit Sophie, but was that simply just a distraction for a man who should know better?

Probably of greater personal pressure in his head had been his contact, his lunches, his coffees with Andrea. Until her death, she had become more and more of a part of his life. Since he had lost her last autumn, he had allowed his mind to wander to Sophie during the couple of times he had come into contact with her: over Christmas at drinks with Jules and her husband Gerald and then again at New Year. But somehow it was just a passing infatuation, a lust after a younger model. With Andrea it had been so much more: a connection, a comfort and always a feeling that his position in his chair had not mattered. He had always found Andrea very attractive, and yet there was so much more to the feelings inside him than simply the physical arousal when they were in close proximity to each other, sharing their personal space.

'Sorry, I don't mean to be unhelpful and I should be more considerate, I have a lot on my plate at work and I know that should not be an excuse, but it kind of fills my head.' Mike knew that Victoria would believe him as she always blamed his work for taking up too much head space.

'Well my business fills my head as well, only it is just for two weeks a year and not 52!' Victoria was starting to calm down a little, perhaps the goods train was approaching an amber light.

Mike did not want to point out he did not work 52 weeks a year and that when they had a break he only checked his emails for an hour or so a day; that approach would merely stoke the boilers of discontent on the train.

When was their last holiday together? Oh yes, how could he forget that fateful trip to France in the car? Paris and then a wander south had sounded so lovely as they had planned it some six years ago. No need to worry about the chair and airports they had agreed. And then the disaster had unfolded.

The puncture on the A13 to Paris and the wait for the man in the van to fix something that Mike was sure Victoria could have helped with if she had been bothered… The car sickness that seemed never to end for Victoria who, only when they were 650 miles into France, announced that she would rather fly everywhere… The hotel they'd booked online that looked as if the Gestapo had only just left it the previous week, rustic charm stretching the description to breaking point… The inevitable hotel change at 3am when Victoria announced she simply could not stay a moment longer in 'this flea pit'…

At least they had found a modern and comfortable hotel

on a golf resort but then Victoria had announced she was flying home two days early so as to avoid the drive. Mike had realised that perhaps this would be their last holiday as a couple.

It could only have been a year or so after that when he had started to enjoy Andrea's company at work. His mind had returned to Andrea yet again. How often it did, he thought to himself.

'You are right, of course, and I did not mean that sarcastically. Why don't you just call the suppliers and check how big your order was last year and what varieties you got in and then we can have a quick chat this evening, it will still be OK if you email them first thing tomorrow.' Mike put on his helpful business advisor voice.

'Finally why don't you just pull off the computer the details of your advanced orders, no doubt Gerald will try and order the most expensive arrangement going?'

Jules' husband, Gerald, worked for a merchant bank. He commuted daily but always caught an earlier train than Mike. They had known each other as a couple for over a decade.

'That is a great idea, thanks darling, I am so sorry I was shitty, but you know how I hate this time of year.' Victoria was back to her usual self.

'She is actually lovely when not stressed,' he thought to himself. 'And here I am thinking of my dead friend again.' A wave of guilt spread over him like a duvet being thrown in the air as a bed is made. It settled to cover his whole body.

'I suspect Gerald only spends so much on flowers as he has such a guilty conscience, Jules is convinced he's playing around again. Apparently his new secretary is a part-time swimwear model!' Victoria was always aware of the latest news from her friends, who seemed to spend more time in her shop drinking coffee than doing anything productive.

'God,' thought Mike, 'two gentlemen with guilt and yet nothing happened with Andrea, I must remember that.'

'Wow, really? I must pop across to the city and have a beer with him one lunchtime and catch a look!' Mike was only joking and Victoria knew it.

'Well love, I am sure if you pushed really hard on those wheels you may even be able to keep up with her long legs as she walks down the street!' Victoria's response whilst accurate was a little hard to take for Mike to take as a joke.

'True darling!'

Mike went back into his head. At least he knew the most that Victoria would throw at him was that he was thinking too much of work.

The countdown to Valentine's Day continued. The extra flowers were ordered in, Sophie was hired for a week for cash in hand and Mike braced himself for the inevitable call at the office on the 13th.

'If only it would fall on a Sunday, then I wouldn't have all this aggravation the day before,' he mused to himself as he sat on the train on Tuesday 12th February. He had been slightly delayed this morning as the cats had managed to miss their dirt box in the utility room and he had spent an extra five minutes cleaning the tiled floor. He'd had no time to grab that cappuccino.

Without the caffeine, Mike felt himself starting to doze off earlier than usual, he would be fast asleep long before Basingstoke.

'Well it is good to see you again.' Andrea was standing in front of him. They were in a busy street – it felt like London but Mike could not make out any landmarks. There seemed to be people all around but they were in a sort of fog, no faces stood out from the crowd, there seemed no definition except Andrea.

'It's a surprise to see you! I thought we were going to meet up again but I was not certain where or when… was I meant to see you in the caravan park place?' Mike felt like he was conducting a business conversation over the location of a meeting, it sounded so matter of fact.

'Caravan park, what are you wittering on about?' Andrea seemed short with him. 'We agreed to see each other here and you are on time.'

'This is really very confusing for me, you'll have to bear with me.' Mike felt off balance in the conversation.

'It's very straightforward,' Andrea continued 'When you are here, you feel more than you see with your eyes; it's very intuitive, the location is moveable, we are static when we are communicating. People here don't seem to speak, we just connect. I realise this all sounds very abstract but it sort of works and is understandable when you get here. There is though a bit of a difference when you feel different sorts of people. I realise that you are only visiting, so to speak, you are not a permanent resident!' Andrea laughed a little with embarrassment. She could not bring herself to call him alive or refer to herself as dead.

'The difference when I am with you is quite startling. You see, you change when you visit, like the fact that you can walk and stand, but somehow that would not necessarily be the same if you were…' Andrea's voice trailed off. There was no way she was going to talk about him dying.

'So how did I connect with you to be here now?' Mike was intrigued and wanted to understand the logistics. He seemed to miss the differences that Andrea intimated at.

'That's a great question and to be honest I don't really know.' Andrea seemed as interested as he was and also pleased she was not being drawn into the whole question of differences between visitors and permanent residents as she saw them.

'Perhaps I just felt the need to connect with you today,' Mike continued. 'Home is a bit stressful and work is the same old crap!'

'That would kind of make sense I guess,' said Andrea.

‘Perhaps we connect when you need someone inside your head to speak with, to share problems. That may trigger our meetings.’

‘Well I have tried to connect with you before, only it hasn’t really worked. Perhaps I need to do so subconsciously if that makes sense.’ Mike was trying to understand it as he was speaking. He had not been thinking of Andrea for a couple of weeks, he had not dreamt again.

‘You’ve had a lot of aggravation recently haven’t you? You and Vicky are not getting on too well.’

‘How the hell do you know that? Are you inside my head or watching over me?’ Mike could not help but sound accusing. Andrea’s statement had taken him by surprise and he tended to respond quickly when he felt threatened, his legal training kicking in.

‘And she hates to be called Vicky, as you bloody well know.’ Mike instantly regretted snapping back.

There was a rush of hot wetness on his legs, he lurched up, slipped and fell against the table in front of him

‘Oh my God I am so sorry!’ A rather large woman with two bags had just managed to spill the majority of her latte. ‘Oh your legs!’ Clearly the woman was in shock at being as insensitive as she saw Mike trying to first steady himself and then move in his customary lurches by gripping the top of the seats.

‘I hope that did not burn you, or perhaps you cannot feel?’

She was going red in the face and clearly digging a hole so large she would never get out.

'Madam, my bones in my legs were shattered in a car accident when I was 21. That does not mean to say that my nerve endings have yet failed! Yes your bloody coffee was hot! My suit is soaked and it will need to be dry cleaned. Your manner, I am assuming, is down to embarrassment at your inability to climb onto a train clasping more than one thing in your fat hands at a time.' At times of stress Mike usually became eloquent and, if Victoria were to be believed, cutting and viscous. 'I suggest you go to the lavatory and fetch as many paper towels as you can so we can stem the tsunami that is flowing across the table.'

The woman did as she was told and after ten minutes of wiping, the area looked almost clean. Mike settled himself into a dry seat and was pleased his suit trousers did not seem to be too wet after the towel drying.

Mike closed his eyes – there were still 15 minutes of travelling before Waterloo. He thought of Andrea. Now why had he snapped at her, was the coffee incident to blame for him waking up or had she left because he has been rude. How could she have left the dream? She was dead and yet he had spoken with her twice while asleep. Was she in my head, or was he able to communicate with the afterlife as long as he was dreaming? Was dreaming the afterlife anyway? Perhaps it was the way people were prepared for it, by experiencing it a little bit all through their lives? If that was the case, then life must seem to just merge into death, with people just spending all their time eventually in the dream state and not in the waking living state?

Questions cascaded through Mike's mind as the train lumbered towards its terminal. How did Andrea distinguish between him as being alive and the other people she met in the afterlife? She said she felt and didn't really see him? Mike wanted so much to see Andrea again, to sit down for a couple of hours and talk through these matters while enjoying the company of his dear friend and confidant.

'I really am most awfully sorry for the suit, I can understand why you were so upset with me. I really should not have said those things, about your legs I mean. Oh and there I have gone and done it again.' The lady was standing up reaching for her bags from the rack over the seats. The train was stationary at Waterloo and people were filing out to start the daily routine of work, meetings, emails, telephone calls… until they could climb back onto the same trains that would whisk them home to a gin and tonic at 6.20pm that night.

'Please don't worry, I'm not feeling myself. I was rude back then and you had been very apologetic, it could have happened to anyone. Let's put it down to experience and try and have a nice day, I shall.' Mike was magnanimous in response. Life was too short to worry and get irritable over such things he thought to himself.

Mike lurched onto the platform on his sticks and the conductor was there with his wheelchair.

'If you don't mind me saying so, you do not look your usual smart self today,' said the conductor as he held the wheelchair whilst Mike lowered himself into it. 'That suit could do with a dry clean.'

CHAPTER 3

WEDNESDAY 13th February arrived and Mike had managed to have enough work to do quietly from home, so that he did not need to go into London. That way he would be on hand for Victoria, although it was a fine balance he had to make. He had to appear to be busy and let her manage her business without interfering, yet be helpful if needed when it all started to get too much for her. At least he would not have the call in his office that he dreaded most years and the rush to catch the quickest train home. His travel arrangements in his wheelchair usually went smoothly, but that was because they had been planned and he gave himself enough time to get around. Charging out of the office and trying to find a cab, then the slalom course around passengers on the concourse at Waterloo were frankly rather stressful for Mike. Working at home and being close were in some ways selfish choices Mike had made to help his wife if he were needed.

'Right then, I am off to the shop.' Victoria was standing in front of him in her usual skinny jeans and top. It was 6.30 in the morning. 'And you're working from home then today? Another case to prepare no doubt. I hope you have not done that on my account. I have Sophie in and so will have everything covered.' She sounded confident and Mike was pleased.

'Of course I haven't changed my diary around to work from home to assist my lovely wife if needed on the busiest day of her year.' Mike wanted to make it sound light-hearted,so Victoria knew she could call on him if needed.

'Thanks, see you later, I'll bring home an Indian take away around 8. Won't be able to face cooking after the day I'll have had.' With that Victoria turned and walked out of the front door, leaving Mike in his chair in the hall.

Mike worked in his study during the morning, topping up with coffee every hour or so. He was pleased with what he had managed to cover by lunchtime. Still no call from Victoria so perhaps everything was going to plan.

Then the mobile started to vibrate. He saw the shop number on the screen.

'Mike, Victoria has asked me to call you.' Sophie's voice sounded young and soft in his ear. 'We could really do with another pair of hands here, it's starting to go a bit crazy, and she wondered how your work was going? If it's OK, I can drive the van back to yours to collect you and you could come down to the shop for the afternoon.'

'Sophie sure, I did everything I needed to and I would have only spent the afternoon on the web.' Mike wasn't lying. He had managed to do all his work, but he had been intending to search online for details of a clinic in Atlanta that had started to carry out some pretty drastic surgery to accident victims. When he had been hurt more than twenty years ago the theory had always been about keeping the limbs and then spending your time in a chair. Now the cutting-edge approach was to amputate and fix prosthetics and have everyone running around like a South African sprinter. Mike did not have long to wait until his lift arrived so he could start his afternoon as a shop assistant.

'The clinic research will have to wait for another day,' he thought to himself as he shut his computer down.

Sophie pulled into the drive and jumped out of the driver's side of the little van, her long blonde hair flowing over her shoulders. Her jeans were tight and the T-shirt even tighter. Mike smiled, that was a sight to lift the spirits of any mid-forties man, he thought to himself.

'Hi Mike. You jump in and I'll fold the chair up and pop it into the back.' Mike was happy to oblige and soon they were driving along the leafy suburban roads on the outskirts of Winchester towards the shop.

'Thanks for helping out Victoria this week.' Mike had

been worried about the pressure on his wife without Sophie on board. Selfishly it relieved him.

'It's fun actually. I was back home studying for a land law paper and if I read about Black Acre or Stokes v Cambridge much more I'll go mad. Also, to be honest the money comes in handy. Uni is rather expensive if you want to get the most out of it and next year I really want to move out of halls and rent with a couple of girlfriends, which will mean more dosh.'

'Sophie, your dad must earn a fortune. Don't kid me you are feeling the recession! I'm sure uni is a struggle for some.' Mike had always had an easy-going relationship with Sophie and seen her grow up. At one stage they had lived just five minutes away, but then Jules and Gerald had moved to a mini country pile in a village about five miles out of Winchester. There were still the regular weekend meets for drinks or BBQs in the summer and Victoria and Jules had their regular Pilates one evening during the week.

'Dad is really concerned that I learn the value of money. He says it will teach me to respect money and work harder. Sometimes I even wonder if he would leave everything to some bloody charity rather than see me inherit! Not that I want Pops dead of course.' She was clearly worried that she had said too much and coloured a little as she tried to cover her embarrassment.

'Well it's difficult for me to comment as Victoria and I have never had children, but it does sound as though your dad has the right approach.' Mike suddenly thought he sounded as though he were over 50. Where had all the years gone?

'I suppose after the accident you couldn't.' Sophie's question did not sound accusing, more factual and Mike did not find himself upset by her apparent insensitivity. She did not seem to think it was too direct as she slowed the van carefully to a stop at a roundabout.

'Actually, it's no real secret, Victoria can't have kids. We tried for years and after we gave up on the different options we got the shop five years ago. VFs is really our little one I suppose!'

'Sorry I didn't realise and just assumed… silly of me really.' Sophie looked a little flushed and Mike felt sorry for her. Perhaps she had just realised how direct she had been.

'Don't worry, not a problem at all.' Mike tapped his hand on her thigh in a comforting way and instantly regretted his actions.

'What are you thinking of you idiot,' he told himself. He felt too relaxed in her company – that was dangerous. Sophie didn't say anything and did not seem to even notice his overfamiliarity. The van pulled up into the car space behind the shop and he climbed into the chair that Sophie had got out of the back. He wished he had not touched her thigh. He was not some dirty old man, he told himself.

'God,' he thought to himself, 'I have enough emotional crap going on trying to maintain a relationship with my dead friend and jump-start my faltering marriage.' Mike realised he had not been consciously thinking about addressing his marriage before. Perhaps all marriages go through a sort of drifting stage after the 20 years that he and Victoria had been together. He knew he should make more of an effort. Being there for Victoria during this busy time was perhaps the first step.

'Right then let's go and play florists!' Mike said as he pushed the chair towards the short ramp that led up to the open back door of the shop. 'Yes I should be here to help Victoria and I am pleased I am, ' he thought to himself. 'Mike if you make an effort then perhaps things will all turn out OK. Andrea is dead, God damn it, Victoria is here, alive and, for most men, still a damn good looking woman.' Mike smiled as he entered the back of the shop

'The 7th cavalry has arrived, darling, just point me in a direction and I shall do whatever!' Mike really wanted to sound enthusiastic and helpful. Victoria turned and looked at him, the bottom of one leg of her jeans was soaked and a bucket that had been full of water was leaning against it with the rest of the contents on the floor. Her hands had scratches on them, her hair had fallen out from his neat bun and she looked about to burst into tears.

'I don't need the fucking 7th cavalry, I need some help from my crippled husband.' With that the tears flooded from Victoria, a damn had been breached by a bouncing bomb and water gushed.

Mike pushed his chair towards her, held out his arms and held his wife. 'Sophie, please get a mop and bucket from by the back door and clear this mess up.' After ten minutes calm was restored and then, after a strong cup of tea, Victoria was back to her normal self, a little stressed but happy with her help around her.

Mike however was left reeling inside. Victoria's comment had hurt, perhaps he rationalised to himself he had been a little insensitive over his charging to the rescue comments, but still 'crippled husband' did sting rather.

The rest of the afternoon passed without much incident, Victoria hurried around the shop looking increasingly flustered and then being calmed by more strong tea. Mike dealt with the paperwork and took phone calls and helped at the counter as much as he could to let Victoria and Sophie make up the flower arrangements.

The following day arrived and Mike had already agreed to take it off and help in the shop. Victoria would be driving around Winchester most of the day with deliveries. His role was to take the money from the people who came in to collect their flowers that had been pre-ordered.

The bouquet for Jules was truly magnificent and was ready to go out in the second delivery run of the day.

'That is a fantastic arrangement for your mum,' Mike commented to Sophie as they arranged the flowers by the back door waiting for Victoria to return in her little van. 'Your dad really knows how to show how much he loves his wife!'

'Well I guess that is one way to guarantee he gets a blowjob from her this evening!' Sophie's candour shocked Mike, who was not a little embarrassed by the thought. Such comments he thought should best be kept for a few drinks after a rugby match at Twickenham.

'Sophie, that's not the approach I would expect from such a well brought up young lady. And frankly I don't care if I sound like I am 60, although I definitely am not!' Mike actually meant it, this was not a conversation he wanted to have. He had been pleased to get up this morning with the idea of helping Victoria out in the shop and he wanted to try and make things work between them. He was not certain how long that feeling would last or even if he would be successful but he knew he was approaching things in the right way. He did not want a personal or sexually charged conversation with a fit young law student.

'I'm sorry Mike, it's just that people seem to get so hung up on sex and love and confuse the shit between them! I know that Mum and Dad have real feelings for each other and have been together for simply decades but we all know that Dad drifts occasionally.'

This was getting too much for Mike. He was having an intimate conversation with a friend's 19-year-old daughter whom he had known since she was a little more than a toddler! What was more, her low cut T-shirt left very little to the imagination as she bent over the flower stands in front of him. He would try and look in a different direction but somehow it was not always easy to pretend to himself he did not enjoy the view.

'Sophie, I really don't want to have this conversation with you. I find it rather embarrassing frankly.'

Sophie looked up and straight into his eyes.

'Sorry, you are right, but I have noticed you are enjoying the view, I thought I would wear this top for you today!'

Mike did not know where to look or what to say and he felt himself going red for the first time in decades. At that moment, he thought his life had been saved when Victoria turned the van in off the road and jumped out.

'Soph, love, a quick coffee please as Mike and I load this lot. Thanks both of you for getting everything to the back door. Don't suppose you got it in delivery order for a sensible route around town?' Victoria was in her organising mood!

The van loaded, Victoria drove off with a cheery wave from the open window. Mike had been so relieved to see his wife arrive and now was dreading being left alone with Sophie in the shop.

In fact, Mike need not have felt so worried, nothing else risqué was said and the day passed pleasantly enough. By the end of the week the madness that had been this year's Valentine's Day had passed into history. Mike was back commuting and he settled down into his seat on the 6.20pm home run on Friday. He was looking forward to opening a bottle of red wine that night and enjoying supper with Victoria before a very lazy weekend. He felt they had deserved it.

'I am sorry I got the hump with you the other day.' Andrea was laying on a bench in a park with a hand wrapped around a glass of red. Mike was sitting at the end of the bench, her hair just touching his trouser leg. He was not stroking her hair or touching her at all. The sun was out and it was warm. He could hear insects and birds but not see anyone else. It was as if they were in a lovely park, there were trees in the distance swaying in the wind. The scenery seemed to roll into undulating partially maintained grounds.

'I am sorry I snapped too, I didn't know if I was woken up with a lap full of coffee or if you had just left because we were both annoyed with each other.' Mike was matter of fact with his reply, a little conciliatory in fact. He wanted to talk without upsetting Andrea.

'I suppose this is just really difficult for you, I can see. I mean I sense everything in your life and I feel sort of protective about you. I like you Mike, a lot, and always have done although we never really got past pleasantries in life.' Andrea seemed at ease in chatting to him.

'Well if you are there all the time, do you feel whatever I am feeling, I mean seeing? If I get angry do you feel angry?' Mike was also feeling far too relaxed in chatting to her, this was the third time he had communicated with his dead friend.

'You're dead though!' Mike blurted it out again without thinking.

'For the love of God, I thought we have got past that point! Yes I am, and yes I enjoy coming back to communicate with you. This is so relaxing, isn't it?' Andrea sipped her glass of wine. 'I do find it a little upsetting when you remind me I'm dead, that word seems so final but when you arrive here you realise that it isn't final at all. I think it works like this, I feel a real connection with you, I want to spend time like this with you, I can sense when you are upset or anxious and I like it when you feel happy. I can feel that now, you are happy now. I would love it if you stroked my hair.'

The last time Mike had touched Andrea in this way, they were alone in their favourite restaurant and he had leaned across the table and tucked her hair behind her ear. That must have been the week before the accident. He leaned down and stroked her hair, it fell across his lap as he did so. It felt silky and smooth, she smelled lovely. Andrea lay there in the sunshine, her lovely sparkling blue eyes hidden from view beneath her eye lids. She was not asleep, but looked so peaceful to Mike.

'That is gorgeous, you deserve a sip of wine as a thank you.' She said as she passed her glass up to him.

'It was a pleasure.' He meant it.

'It's funny, but when I'm dreaming with you my legs are

always fine. In the normal world, I can't cope with anyone leaning against my legs like this, the pressure you know. But here it does not seem to affect me. I can walk, stand without help and even now have you pressing against my thigh and it is not an issue.'

'Funnily enough I have never seen you in a wheelchair.' Andrea meant what she said. 'I saw the person, the confident, articulate man, the man in control, I never saw the disability'

Mike was struggling with how to respond. Perhaps it was the wine, he felt so very flattered, and he couldn't remember a time when someone had described him like that. It felt good.

'Do you know how time works here?' Mike asked, as he thought perhaps at some point he would have to wake up. He couldn't rely upon another woman spilling coffee in his lap.

'Not really, no! Although I guess that's not the answer you want to hear.' Andrea was trying to be helpful but appreciated her lack of knowledge. 'Time is a little like sight here. Like I said, you don't really see someone, you sense them. Equally, you don't know how long things take, whatever you're doing somehow fills the space you have available in time. You don't know how many minutes or hours, it just takes that long. I'm beginning to realise that being dead – there, I've used the word myself – is just like being alive, only dreaming. You don't really understand how long things take in dreams do you, you just dream.'

'I appreciate I have not been that happy recently.' Mike

volunteered all of a sudden. 'I did find it difficult with Victoria's friend's daughter walking around in the shop. I have never strayed from Victoria and then I start to feel guilty about our relationship. Is this straying, do you think? After all, it's all in my head. That has just sounded so jumbled up! And I know we saw each other in the office and we enjoyed each other's company, but nothing ever really happened, I mean did it?'

'I suppose it depends upon how you describe the relationship we have. I am no threat to Victoria on a physical basis but I sense you would rather spend your time with me here than with her. And I do know you haven't told her about me.' Andrea was alarmingly accurate for Mike. 'I don't really understand why you haven't mentioned our meetings, I guess it is a little difficult to explain to your wife that you enjoy spending time with your friend in the afterlife. There, that's a much nicer way of putting it, isn't it, than dead friend?'

Andrea smiled and Mike felt as though his whole life had instantly improved by just seeing her radiant face. Her eyes twinkled with happiness. 'I guess,' Andrea continued, 'that it was somehow more difficult to explain our relationship when we saw each other most days and were, let's be honest, becoming increasingly fond of each other. Now it should be easier to chat to Victoria about your dreams, because that is all I am, a dream.'

'Oh Andrea, I just don't know.' Mike felt confused and

worried. 'In life we let things get too far, although we never actually… well you know!' Mike thought he sounded like a teenager and hated himself for it. 'And now I somehow feel even closer to you and want you even more. Frankly I think I need some help or another glass of red!' Mike wanted to lighten the mood in the conversation.

'As for Sophie, I think you should be careful there. I appreciate she is rather tempting but there is something a bit dangerous and that worries me on your behalf.' Andrea said as she held out her hand for the return of the glass of red. Mike had drained nearly half of the large glass.

'Well I hardly think that is helping me. I appreciate your warning, but Sophie is not my main concern right now. I can control my base animal instincts! Well just!' Mike smiled, he was more concerned with the confusion he felt over his wife and Andrea.

'Shall we walk on the grass?' Andrea asked. As they both stood Mike felt completely normal walking along, their hands casually touched as their arms gently swayed. Mike noticed the glass had gone.

'What happened to the glass of red?' He was intrigued.

'When you've finished with things here they simply vanish. It's actually rather useful.' Andrea had now reached for his hand and their fingers loosely entwined. Mike felt very safe all of a sudden, as though nothing else could harm him.

'The view is to die for, the rolling grass meadow and those

trees in the valley over there to the right.' Mike and Andrea had stopped and they stood close together drinking in the scene.

'Unfortunate choice of phrase, my dear!' Andrea had a wry smile on her face.

'Fuck, that was not very tactful of me!' Mike was pleased to see Andrea was seeing the funny side of his terminology.

'I'm sorry but we are going to have to call it a day for now,' said Andrea as she turned towards him. 'We'll see each other again very soon.'

With that Andrea melted away, becoming part of the beautiful scene. Their hands slipping apart, leaving Mike alone.

Instantly Mike missed her, he missed her closeness, her hand in his. He missed looking into those lovely eyes. He missed that feeling of safety, security… of home.

'Darling, I am so sorry, I must have fallen asleep on the train.' Mike was on his mobile phone to Victoria, he was sitting in his wheelchair on the platform at Southampton Parkway, the next stop after Winchester. He was feeling flustered and guilty.

'You never fall asleep for that long! I hope you've not been drinking on the train again? You promised me that was a habit you were going to stop.' Victoria was clearly not in a very understanding mood.

'No I haven't!' Mike was livid at being treated like a

teenager. However he knew it was his fault for falling asleep and he did not want the weekend to start with a row. 'I'll grab a cab straight back home and we can collect the car tomorrow morning from Winchester station.'

'Whatever! I've made a lovely dinner as a thank you for all your help this week. I'll see if I can rescue it. See you in 45 minutes or so.'

Victoria put the phone down, walked across the kitchen and pored herself a large glass of white wine from the fridge. Mike had been acting strangely lately, he never overslept on the train home. She felt annoyed that he would not appreciate the trouble she had been to by way of thanks for all his support this week. 'You never know,' she thought to herself after a nice meal, a bottle of wine perhaps we could have found some of that old intimacy.' Victoria drained a large mouthful of the chilled white. 'Why should I make all the bloody effort?' She thought, as she looked at the tagine bubbling away with Chicken and preserved lemons on the range cooker.

Back at Southampton Mike pushed himself to the taxi rank. Why did he feel so bad, all he had done was fall asleep and have a dream, yet he felt he had been so disloyal to Victoria? He had a friend who was dead, and even when she was alive they had never got past an intimate lunch, for God sake, so why did he feel so bad?

'Winchester, please mate' Mike said as he approached the first cab in the row. '18 Priory Place - it's just off the Stockbridge Road. I can give you directions when we're nearly there.'

The journey didn't take long. On arrival Mike paid the cab driver and pushed himself in his wheelchair up the drive to the front door.

'I am so sorry, I was short with you,' Victoria said as she opened the door. She stood there looking lovely and Mike was relieved. 'I know you don't drink on the train coming home any more and even if you had then I shouldn't have questioned it. After all I hope I am your wife not your mother.' Victoria had mellowed with her wine and although would not admit it the dinner had needed the extra slow heat over the last 40 minutes to really marinate the flavours. The smell of Morocco wafted out of the front door to greet Mike along with his wife.

'I am sorry too, darling, I just feel asleep.' Victoria bent down and kissed him, their lips brushed together

'Hang on I can smell red wine! Mike I don't care if you had a glass, I just said that but why did you have to lie to me?' Victoria had straightened up and was instantly angry with him.

'I didn't have a bloody glass of wine! I feel asleep, I have apologised already, I am sorry about dinner, I am sure it will still be lovely.' Mike was feeling guiltier with every syllable that he uttered. How could the taste possibly come from his dream? It was a dream wasn't it? Had he just been in the afterlife as Andrea had put it? In which case how did he manage to cross between the two?

Mike felt confused and guilty. The time he had spent with Andrea had been lovely and suddenly he was being brought back down to earth with a bump, and he didn't like it.

Mike pushed himself into the house and straight into the kitchen where the table was set for dinner. A bottle of red was open on the table. He poured himself out a glass and took a long swig. This evening could go either way, it hung in the balance between the row from hell and companionable silence interspersed with a few pleasantries before bed.

The companionable silence reigned. Mike wanted to say sorry, to tell Victoria he had not drunk red wine, to explain his dream, perhaps even it was time to explain to his wife that he had always been faithful, but had enjoyed Andrea's company but that he now missed her so much it hurt inside. Mike wanted to make it work with Victoria, but how could he when she knew nothing of that private side of his life. Did she need to know, and even if she didn't, why did he feel a need to tell her? To unburden his soul, to put things behind him and try and enjoy the life he had with his wife.

Victoria drank her white wine and talked of the takings from the shop that week. A better year than the last – she was speaking as though she were a parent, proud of the accomplishment of her child who, having spent hours of time being ferried around for some club or other had now performed at their best in competition and all that support had now paid off. The empty white wine bottle clinked in the bag in the utility room to be taken for recycling over the weekend – by 11pm it had been drained by Victoria, who felt she had deserved the treat after such a week.

CHAPTER 4

THE FOLLOWING week passed without incident. For Mike this meant he did not dream about Andrea. He got up, he left the house, he commuted, he worked and he came home. Life post Valentine's Day settled back as it should. Victoria was content and they seemed to rub along. Victoria had not mentioned the wine again from Mike's train trip but he noticed when they kissed in the evening she seemed to let her lips linger a little longer than usual, was she being loving or checking up on him?

What was it his old boss from all those years had said? 'Only the paranoid survive?' Well if he was being paranoid, he really had no need to be. Without dreaming of Andrea he had no need to worry about having an illicit glass of wine be it in this life or the next.

'I had Jules come in the shop today.' They were organising dinner. It was a Thursday evening and Mike was stirring the pasta sauce on the hob. Victoria was laying the table. 'She wondered if you could help Sophie with some law paper thing. I said you would be delighted, I didn't mention the fact that you struggled to keep your eyes off her when she helps me out in the shop.'

'Yes she is pretty but I don't think I'm some sort of pervert!' Mike was more than a little affronted by his wife's comments. He remembered how relieved he had been when she had arrived at the shop in the van when Sophie had, as far as Mike was concerned, crossed a line in their last conversation together.

'Well I forgot to text you at work today, sorry! She is coming over around 7.30 tonight.' Victoria sounded as though she did not care about changing whatever Mike's arrangements had been for that evening. 'I'll be off at the Pilates class but should be back around 10 after a drink with Jules. Try not to get into any trouble'

'I won't get into trouble thank you and frankly I would rather stay in and watch the football with a couple of beers.' Mike was feeling uncomfortable at the very thought of Sophie coming over without Victoria around and while he was not the greatest sports fan he would have preferred to have the evening he had planned rather than the one his wife had organised without checking with him first. 'In fact can you please contact her and let her know it is simply not convenient. I mean, bloody hell darling, I really don't like having things sprung on me, you know that.'

'Me thinks you protest too much sweetie. Well I am sure you will not chase her around in your wheelchair!' Victoria seemed oblivious to Mike's irritation over the evening. 'Although that is very nice of you to call me darling, you have not done that for some time.'

'Well,' thought Mike 'Perhaps we have started to turn a corner after Valentine's Day and if that's the case, helping out Sophie tonight may be just another step along the way.'

'OK, as usual I shall agree!' Mike had wanted to sound conciliatory and magnanimous, but, somehow unusually for him, it had come out quite wrong.

'Thank you, I did say I was sorry for forgetting to text you and I had promised Jules you would help her, I really didn't think it would be such an inconvenience.' Victoria sounded grateful to Mike.

Just as dinner was finished, right on time they heard a car pull up on the drive. 'Your young lady has arrived!' Victoria clearly could not care how her remarks were affecting Mike. 'And thank you again for helping her.' Victoria's afterthought had eased her initial comment.

'Come on in Sophie, Mike's in the kitchen. I have to go off to Pilates so you two can bore yourselves silly with land law.' Victoria brushed past Sophie in the hall and Mike heard the front door close behind her just as she was saying, 'Love you darling!'

Sophie walked into the kitchen. She was in jeans and a wax jacket that looked as though it covered some sort of university sweatshirt hoody top and she had a rucksack which was casually hanging from her left shoulder. Mike turned his wheelchair to face her.

'Hi Sophie! I'm sorry, Victoria forgot to let me know during the day that you would be popping in. I'm happy to help but I'm afraid all my text books are at the office. We can always look things up online though. I'll go and get the laptop. We can work in the kitchen, it's the best room for wireless.' Mike sounded friendly and at the same time business-like. He had no wish to come across as brusque, but neither did he want any embarrassment.

Sophie smiled at him 'Thanks Mike, I owe you for helping me with this sudden assignment. Shall I pop the dishes by the sink to clear the table?'

'Great thanks,' said Mike as he pushed himself passed her towards the hallway so he could recover his laptop from the study.

In a couple of moments Mike was back, laptop on his lap. Sophie turned from the sink where she had just left the last of the pasta dishes. Mike pushed himself to the table, popped the laptop on to it and opened it up.

'OK, so where is this dreaded assignment then?' Mike asked. He was starting to relax, maybe this was not going to be too bad after all. Perhaps if he managed to get through matters quickly he may even get to see the second half of the match. Sophie reached into her rucksack and pulled out a file containing a word processed document several pages long.

'Well this is how far I have got, could you take a look and let me know if I have covered all the Law of Property Act stuff from 1925. It is all on 146 notice procedures.' Sophie passed Mike the papers. 'Shall I pop the kettle on while you read?' Sophie did not wait for an answer but started to move towards the kettle.

'Sure, thanks, I would prefer a beer but I suppose we have to keep clear heads.' Mike opened the papers and started to read. He did not look up as Sophie removed her jacket and put it across the back of one of the kitchen chairs.

By the time the kettle had boiled and Sophie set down two cups of tea on the table Mike had speed-read about half the document.

'This is first-class Sophie, you're a bright kid,' Mike said, before adding, 'sorry that sounded patronising – I didn't mean it. This is really very good. As long as you bring in the effect of the 2002 Act in the next part you have this licked.' Mike really was impressed, perhaps he would have to consider offering Sophie a placement with his firm after her degree. Gerald had raised the issue with him during the Christmas drinks and he had skirted around it. He disliked his arm being twisted by a friend for a favour, but having read her work, perhaps he thought she could justify a place on merit.

Whether Gerald would see it that way would be a different matter…

'Thanks, I did try and cover most of the points.' Sophie was sitting next to Mike. 'I think I did the bit about that Act on page nine.' Sophie leant across Mike and turned the pages. Mike suddenly became aware of how close she was and he stopped being engrossed in the law and realised her breasts were brushing his arm.

'Well let us just read that part, then.' Mike started to feel uncomfortable all over again, just like Valentine's Day at the shop. Only this time there would be no Victoria arriving in the little van to save him, at least certainly not for the next hour or more.

'Sophie this is fine,' Mike said as he finished the page. 'In fact there really is no need for me to look at it.' Mike started to worry if Sophie's visit had been a ruse all along, on a night when she would know that Victoria would be out. 'No, don't be ridiculous, you are paranoid,' he said to himself. Nevertheless he had a very uncomfortable feeling in the pit of his stomach.

'Actually I thought it would be OK, but I do value your time in looking through it. I shall come clean, it was a bit of an excuse to come across tonight as I knew Victoria would be out at Pilates with Mum.' Sophie looked too confident for Mike's liking. He shifted uneasily in his wheelchair.

'Oh God,' he thought to himself. 'I just do not want to be

here.' What Mike was not so certain of was why he did not want to be there. Was it because he did not trust himself? Was Sophie too tempting for this average middle-aged man?

'There is a new approach at uni that myself and a few other girls are following or should I say trying to follow. It is called the Sugar Daddy System.' Mike wished he could get up and walk out of the room but he couldn't!

'OK, Sophie I have no idea where this is going, but I don't like the sound of it. I am very happily married.' Mike did not know what Sophie was going to be saying next and he wondered why he had just said that about his marriage. Was he really happily married, and even if he was not, he was still uncomfortable in the extreme with this situation.

'How often do you have sex, Mike?' Sophie said it in a matter of fact tone, not accusing, just enquiring.

'For God's sake, Sophie, I was not happy with our conversation in the shop on Valentine's Day and this is going far beyond the pale! I have no intention of answering that. I suggest you pop your coat on and get going, young lady!' Mike wanted to sound patronising, he hoped it would put an end to this situation.

Sophie did not move from her chair.

'I am going back to uni tomorrow, I have a big party to enjoy on Saturday night and then we hand in this land law assignment on Monday. I have only got this evening to speak with you and explain.' Sophie was now in full flow, Mike realised nothing was going to stop whatever was about to come out of her mouth.

'It goes like this, we girls are all hard up students and fed up with doing shit jobs in the holidays when we want to be in the sunshine reading a good book. So we thought if we each found a nice older man, just one each, who would be willing to support us with a retainer of, say, a few hundred a month, we could then perform certain tasks for that gentleman in return. By default we are looking for a man who is older as I say, not at uni so we can have our fun without ties, but when we all go home to our parents we could repay the gentlemen's… umm... generosity.'

'Jesus, Sophie you are talking about prostitution! For God's sake, I'm speechless. I have a good mind to ring up your father right now.' Mike had been worried about Sophie offering sex on a plate, he had not expected her to be asking for money for it!

'Dad is up at some do in London and staying in the Dorchester, probably with his latest squeeze and Mum, as you know, is at Pilates with your wife.'

'Wife… that's right, my wife, Sophie!' Mike grasped upon her words like a life ring tossed to a drowning man in the ocean.

'I know this is a bit of a shock to you, perhaps think about it and we could firm up arrangements over Easter if you want. As for telling my parents I don't think you will as I shall just tell them you can't stop staring at my tits when I help out in the shop! I shall also say that you have made it all up. I think they'll believe me. After all what would be more normal than a middle-aged man checking out a girl half his age!'

Mike was lost, actually lost for words. He was usually so articulate in awkward moments, but he did not know what to say, even worse he did not know where to look. At that moment Sophie stood up and in one swift movement peeled her top over her head to reveal her pert smooth breasts held in a black lacy bra.

'Look, you should see what you get for your money! I was thinking about £500 a month and you get this when I am home.' She started to reach behind to unclip her bra. Mike could not stop watching, he also felt his groin starting to stir in his trousers and he had to admit to himself he couldn't remember the last time he had had sex. It was probably not even that year.

'Oh shit, Sophie!' He was starting to lose the will to argue and yet he knew this was wrong.

'As I see it, this is not prostitution, I would rather think of it as exclusive access, like a courtesan in medieval Italy.' Sophie paused, 'I reckon you are enjoying this.' Sophie had unclipped her bra and as she finished her sentence let it fall casually to the floor. Her breasts were full, pert and a matter of three feet from Mike's face.

She did not touch her jeans, which Mike was relieved to

notice, as he had assumed that they were the next item of clothing to be dispensed with. Instead she knelt down in front of his wheelchair and looked up into his eyes.

'Oh fuck!' He exclaimed as she started to run her hand over his crotch, which was bulging against his trousers. His head fell back against the back of the chair and he closed his eyes.

'I always swallow,' Sophie said in a low voice as her hand continued to rub his erection through his trousers.

'You're a better man than this, Mike.' Andrea's voice was clear and calm. Mike opened his eyes and pushed his wheelchair back with a lurch.

'No, this is not going to happen.' He felt angry, with himself and with Sophie. 'Get dressed and get out.'

Sophie was still kneeling on the floor but the sudden movement of his chair had made her fall forward and her hands were now palm down on the slate kitchen floor. She was all but on all fours. She looked up at him and started to prowl towards him.

The key in the lock was unmistakable as was the cheery voice from the front door that announced Victoria's early arrival.

'Hi guys, still hard at it? Pilates was fun but I was too tired to go out for a drink with the girls afterwards.' Victoria dropped her bags in the hall and started to walk down the corridor to the kitchen. Sophie stood up and had just pulled her top back on, minus her bra when Mike's wife came through the kitchen door.

Mike was sat in his wheelchair feeling relieved and so happy to see his wife. Then a wave of guilt crashed over his body. Guilt because he had enjoyed watching Sophie strip in front of him. Guilt because he had needed to listen to his dead friend and not his own moral compass. That had seemed to have been misplaced as Sophie's bra had fallen to the floor. Nothing had happened he told himself and what is more, I stopped it. Although had Andrea stopped it and saved him, he wondered.

'We had finished actually, Victoria, Mike was a wonderful help and he has promised I can use him during Easter holidays as much as I like.' Sophie stood in the kitchen as though nothing in the world was wrong. Mike could not help but marvel at her performance as the studious law undergraduate. Perhaps she should have gone to drama school instead?

'Well, I am very pleased to hear it. You know you are welcome over here whenever you like Sophie. In fact I may find you some extra work in the shop during the holidays, I am sure you students are always in need of a few more quid,' Victoria said.

'Money does make a difference to how much you can enjoy uni.' Sophie turned and Mike was sure she quickly winked at him just as Victoria had walked across the kitchen towards the kettle and was out of her eye line.

'I will be going then, Mike thanks again you were… enormous… ly helpful!' And with that Sophie picked up her rucksack and casually walked out of the kitchen into the hall and towards the front door.

'Bye Sophie… happy to help.' Mike just managed to control his voice and then when he thought his evening could not get any worse he spotted her bra laying where it had fallen just under the kitchen table. Because the floor was black slate it did not stand out. Mike felt sick. There was no other word to describe it, he felt sick. He pushed himself around the table and parked himself over the discarded underwear just as Victoria turned around with two cups of tea.

'Bye Sophie! Do you want the tea in here or are you going to watch the telly?' Victoria asked.

'Bye guys!' Came Sophie's cheery answer, as they heard the front door close behind their guest.

'I am tempted to take mine to bed and start reading that new book. I really don't know why but I feel shattered,' said Victoria as she turned to make towards the kitchen door.

'Oh God, please leave the room!' Thought Mike. 'OK darling whatever you want. I'll probably just check a couple of things online as I have the laptop set up. I'll join you in a minute.'

Victoria placed Mike's tea down on the table in front of him, she bent down and gave him a peck on his cheek. 'You're a nice man Mike Stapleford, thanks for helping out Sophie and I am sorry I forgot to warn you.' Victoria straightened up and started to walk to the door. 'Try not to be too long, would be nice to have a cuddle.' She smiled at him and turned and left the kitchen.

Mike reached down from his chair and picked up Sophie's bra, it was black, lacy and he could not help but look at the size, 32D. God, no wonder they looked so lovely.

Then he remembered Andrea. She had saved him, he needed to thank her. He wished that he would see her soon in his dreams. What was important was that nothing had happened with Sophie. He should have a clear conscience yet however hard he tried to run that argument in his head he knew that if Andrea had not spoken to him he would have lost the moral fight with dealing with his courtesan.

He tucked the bra into his laptop bag together with the laptop itself and pushed himself into the study where he left it in its usual position on the floor by the door.

'I have finished sweetie,' he said as he arrived at their bedroom door, he had gone back into the kitchen and collected his tea which he had balanced on a tray in his lap.

Victoria was in bed the book laid open on her lap her head was leaning against the pillows she was propped up but fast asleep. Mike was relieved. He wanted to fall asleep and dream about Andrea, to thank her for being there when he needed her, for rescuing him. The last thing he wanted was to cuddle his wife.

He laid back in bed and closed his eyes, he drifted off to sleep. Andrea was standing in an art gallery of sorts. Other people were there only their faces were indistinguishable. She looked sharp, her eyes flashed from picture to picture across the walls. The ceilings were high and the space felt light and airy. She was wearing a wraparound silk dress which hugged her figure, it was patterned with a base colour of blue, which showed off her eyes.

'How could I have even been tempted with Sophie when she looks so lovely?' He thought to himself.

He walked slowly across the room consuming her with his eyes.

'Thank you so much,' he said, almost in a whisper in her ear as he reached her. She did not turn to face him, but continued to study the picture in front of her. She slipped an arm around his waist and pulled him closer to her.

'You're welcome, my darling, 'she said. 'I knew you were in trouble and can understand your temptation. Was it Oscar Wilde who said, "I can resist everything except temptation"?'

'I think your right. I feel very guilty for getting myself into that position, you had warned me. I suppose I was feeling rather flattered that such an attractive young lady was showing me any sort of attention. I wish I could just tell Victoria about her but I almost don't know where to begin.' Mike was relieved to be able to talk this through with Andrea.

'I think if you had a solid relationship with Victoria then

it would not be a problem. And I shall try and point this out gently, darling, but at the risk of pricking your balloon, I don't think Sophie was interested in you, rather your wallet!' Andrea went on. 'I don't feel threatened by Sophie, in fact I just feel very protective of you and don't want you hurt by either Sophie or for that matter by the backlash from Victoria. Perhaps Vicky, sorry Victoria, is not as secure in her relationship with you as she should be.'

'You know, tonight is the first time I have been able to visit you when I wanted to,' said Mike. 'Usually I just dream and you appear and that is lovely. But this evening I went to sleep and wanted to see you, to thank you. I almost asked my subconscious to bring me here. Of course that's supposing it is my subconscious that has brought me here! Actually you know what, this just gets so confusing when you start to think about it.' Mike felt as though he was tying himself up in knots.

'I see what you mean,' Andrea volunteered helpfully. 'Usually we connect by more luck than judgement, as far as you're concerned, but tonight you sort of made it happen as you wanted to say thank you.'

'That's it entirely. How do you think that works then? And while we are chatting I should point out that Victoria smelt the wine on me that we shared the other day. I had fallen asleep on the train and we met in the park and shared a glass of red.'

'I remember Michael, it was a magical day for me, you

stroked my hair. It was divine.' Andrea looked at a painting in front of her of a lovely rural scene, they were still in the gallery. 'Would you like to visit that place?' She said, as she nodded towards the picture they were standing in front of. They still stood close together with their arms wrapped around each other's waists.

'That would be lovely. It is so great spending time with you.' With that the gallery seemed to melt away and they were standing in the scenery that a moment ago had been the picture.

'That's a bit bloody Harry Potter-esque!' Said Mike. He liked the idea that they were now alone and in fresh air and warm sunshine.

'I suppose it is really. I have no idea how Victoria smelt the wine on you the other night. I did tell you right at the start they don't give you a manual here!' Andrea laughed a little. 'Perhaps in future we'll have to be more careful.' She stopped and thought for a moment 'God doesn't that make it sound like we are trying to cover something up? I suppose I could be considered the other woman!'

'Well to be honest I don't know what I feel guiltier about, being propositioned by a 19-year-old with breasts to die for or spending time with you. Either way, I'm being disloyal to Victoria.'

'You know Mike, sweetie, just because we are not all 19 something does not stop us having nice breasts.' Andrea was smiling but Mike realised that underlying her comment was a tone that very nicely put him in his place. He also made a mental note to try and not look at her cleavage, at least for the time this encounter lasted.

'What's more,' she continued, 'it is far nicer to have a balanced relationship where one can talk, and walk, listen and laugh together as well as having a physical dimension. I think you would quickly get bored of whatever sort of relationship you had with Sophie. And I guess you would also end up being quite a lot poorer!'

'Bloody hell, you really do know everything that goes on. So you knew she wanted to be paid £500 a month?'

'Well I knew she wanted money but not the amount. I didn't know in advance what she intended to do, I am not a clairvoyant! When I warned you to be careful, I just knew she was up to something.'

'That type of relationship you described, about enjoying each other's company as well as the physical side, well I thought that was what I had with Victoria. Only to be honest the physical side sorted of died out after trying for the family. And now well we sort of have our own lives. That probably sounds rather lame, but I commute, work and spend my life in my chair and she lives for her shop. In fact we have not even been away on holiday together for nearly five years.'

'Why don't you go away together?' Andrea was surprised. 'I remember you having leave from the office.'

'Well I took time off. Usually Victoria would take a trip with her friend Jules to some sunshine and spend it by the pool drinking white wine. My old Mum would pop down from Somerset and spend the time with me. I lost my dad years ago and Mum now lives in one of these retirement complexes. She enjoys the change of scenery and it's easier to stay put at home, as it's all fitted out for the chair as opposed to me visiting her.'

'So no sun, sand and sex for Michael!' Said Andrea with a smile.

'No, none! I could bore you silly with the tale of woe that was our road trip through France, which was our last attempt at a holiday together. To be honest, I've looked forward to those visits by my Mum more and more over recent years. I kind of like my own space at home. That probably tells you something.'

'Oh, Mike, it tells me that I want to hug you, to hold you, to care for you. To be honest I don't really know what happens here when I am not with you. It is as though in these times I am alive and sleeping the rest, although I am aware of you and what is happening in your life.' Andrea moved to be even closer to him. He was aware of her silk dress brushing against his arm, he realised he was in a short sleeved shirt and felt warm in the sunshine.

'We have never really held each other as closely as this.' Mike was struggling with his feelings, he wanted to feel her body pressed against his, he wanted to feel her warmth and to wrap his arms around her and snuggle his head into her neck among those long blonde curls.

Andrea turned to face him, she looked into his eyes and he was lost. After they embraced, Mike felt a happiness wash over him, a level of contentment that he could not remember having before. Perhaps it was the lovely feeling of being able to stand and embrace someone he loved without falling over. He certainly did not miss his chair. Love, that was the first time he had got that far, did he love Andrea? Was he falling for her in this life or was he perhaps falling for the life and the chance to walk and stand?

'Mike, you seem miles away. It was just a hug, and I hope we have not overstepped the mark.' Andrea looked concerned.

'For me, that was so much more than a hug. I felt I had come home and that I never wanted to leave.' Mike looked into those piercing blue eyes. He did not feel guilty where Victoria was concerned, although he knew he should. All he wanted to do now was to hold Andrea close again and to kiss those beautiful lips that he could not stop staring at.

'Oh God, Mike, this is starting to gather a momentum way beyond what is good for either of us. We are divided by life and yet it feels so special.'

Mike was feeling his heart beat faster and he felt electricity between them both. In life they had been close colleagues, enjoyed each other's company, but somehow these dreams had brought a level of closeness that seemed to bring contentment to both of them. What was clear was that the feelings were growing and were mutual.

'Well I hope we can meet again really soon, perhaps I shall start to be able to dream at will, and then I have to tell you I will want to see you so much more! Do you think we could start to plan dates? I would like to go on a picnic to the seaside!' Mike felt elated at the thought of being by the sea, enjoying the warmth of the sunshine and having some pate, French bread and red wine.

'Steady,' he thought to himself, 'I am planning a date, planning the menu and all this with my dead girlfriend! Is she my girlfriend?' At mid-40s Mike felt a little self-conscious over such descriptions. They should be confined to people in their 20s he thought. What was clear to him, however, was he didn't want to part from her, he didn't want to wake up. In this life, he felt more complete and happier than he could ever remember feeling in his real life. But then he thought to himself: 'Which is real?' Just because his logical mind told him he was dreaming and that when he woke he would be in his real life, did that make it real? Perhaps if he were true to himself, he would rather be in this life with Andrea where he was happiest.

'Mike I am sensing something.' Andrea was looking straight at his eyes. 'Whatever we say to each other we are separated, we can spend some lovely moments together but you must promise me you will never do anything rash.'

'I have absolutely no idea what you are talking about.' He lied and he knew she realised.

'Please don't lie, I can feel what you feel Mike. I know you are happier here, standing, walking, spending time with me but this is not the real world. Do not get confused between life and death Mike. This is not the Matrix, you know, where everything is turned upside down.' Andrea had stepped away and was holding both his hands at arm's length.

'It is just that I adore this time with you, I love what we do together, our walks, the places we find ourselves in. You cannot realise how wonderful it feels to be able to walk with you holding your hand.'

'Mike all those things can continue, after all I am not about to go anywhere.' Andrea smiled 'Are you sure you don't just love the idea of the freedom you get in this life?'

'No!' Mike felt a little affronted. 'It's great, sure, but so are you and please don't denigrate what we have here, it is so special.' Andrea smiled back at him, drew him close to her and kissed him tenderly, squarely on his lips.

'Now remember darling, what we have is lovely, is special, but you are just a visitor and as such you don't see or feel as I do here. Let us keep to the times like this we have together.' Andrea looked long onto his eyes, he felt them drill into his heart, he felt as though she were trying to imprint a message on him without spelling out the detail.

'Take care, Mike.' And with that Andrea vanished.

CHAPTER 5

THE FOLLOWING morning Mike awoke with a warm contented feeling inside. It felt special that he had been able to spend such a long time with Andrea, particularly as he had been able to make it happen. How he had travelled in his mind to the next world for the night was beyond him. Indeed he was still not sure if it was the next world or just his dreams. In fact were the two the same or was there some sort of parallel universe going on where the dream world seemed to overlap into the next world? And then, there was that conversation with Andrea over which was the real world. He tried to move his legs, they felt heavy and awkward. 'This must be the real world,' he thought to himself. 'Stuck in a wheelchair and stuck in my marriage.'

Still, however the dream contact worked, he felt pleased that it did. Victoria was fast asleep next to him, turned away from him, facing the window. He moved to the side of the bed to swing himself up, and then reached out for the little table so he could steady himself. Just then Victoria rolled over and just caught sight of his thin legs as he started to rise out of a seating position. Mike fell forward and hit his head against the table.

'Shit that hurt!' Mike was rubbing his hand on his head expecting to see blood but his hand was dry.

'That is certainly one way to make you wake up straight away!' Andrea was standing next to him holding his arm and looking to steady him as he swayed slightly on his legs.

'Am I back dreaming?' Mike asked still feeling a little dazed.

'Well you are with me and not Victoria so you must be passed out on your bedroom floor in real life.' Andrea looked concerned for him but also in a way rather pleased he was there with her.

'It is funny when you refer to real life and this is not. I know I am dreaming when I am with you, but it is so lovely I feel a little more comfortable here than I do there.' Mike now felt OK to start to wander. They casually held hands as though it was the most natural thing in the world to do and walked gently downhill. They were in a pine forest. The gradient was not steep and there was a smell of sea air in the breeze, Mike wondered if they were walking down towards a beach.

'You need to be careful Mike, I mean it.' Andrea was sounding surprisingly serious. 'For me I spend all my time here, I have no choice but you are still alive Mike, you visit when you want or can. We spoke about this yesterday. There are parts of this life, if that is what it is, that are great, but there are certain parts that are not very pleasant. You see, you and I have this relationship because you are just a visitor, but if you were, shall we say, a permanent resident, then it would be different between us.'

'I know you keep trying to warn me off but it seems funny to think of time here as not being so lovely when I compare it with life at home," said Mike. 'How do you know I am just visiting now? I may have banged my head so badly I may be dead.' Even as Mike said it he felt relaxed, as though he could accept his end and start a new life.

'I know you are still alive because I can feel these things, I do keep telling you! Perhaps if you started to take more notice of what I say and spent less time trying to work out how to justify being dead and therefore with me, you could understand and accept what we have, when we have it.' Andrea was sounding a little strained, as though she was tired of explaining herself.

'Mike I know we have something very special, but there are parts of this world that you don't realise yet. You will when you are dead and they come with some pretty big disadvantages.'

'Will I still be able to stand, walk and be with you?' Mike felt he needed answers and quickly.

'Mike that is not for now. Now you belong your wife and not with me. You belong in the world that is living and not with the dead.' Andrea was dismissing him as gently as she could.

'Mike, Mike, oh my God are you alright? Mike, Mike can you hear me?' Victoria was crouching beside him, her face streaked with tears, she was brushing his hair off his forehead with a damp sponge. He felt warm blood trickling down his face in between the wipes with the sponge.

'Jesus darling, are you trying to kill me off?' Mike did not feel relieved either to be alive or to be seeing Victoria. He somehow felt cheated he could not spend the day with Andrea.

'Oh God, you're back with me. I was just about to call the ambulance! I feel terrible, I am so sorry darling.' Victoria sounded genuinely upset.

'I wonder if she would be this worried if she realised I nearly had sex with her best friend's 19-year-old daughter last night?' Mike wondered to himself as he hauled his body up against the bed and sat propped against it on the floor. The blood had stopped and he was not feeling too bad.

'I'm OK now darling, please don't worry. I'll start to get ready and just catch a later train.' Mike did not want to make a great deal of fuss, he had his favourite client coming in for a lunch appointment and as it was Friday, they could enjoy a bottle of wine and relax.

'Don't be such a bloody idiot.' Victoria was incensed. 'You have just smashed your head, you could have concussion, and you need to get yourself checked out by a doctor. If you think you are putting that fucking office first today you have another thing coming. In fact I shall go and get your Blackberry now and you can email them.'

With that Victoria stood up and started to walk down the corridor. 'Is it in the laptop bag as usual?' She called as she reached the study.

Mike felt powerless for the first time he could remember. He remained sat on the floor, he tried to mentally prepare himself for the tsunami that was about to engulf his whole life. He did not even know whether to try to lie or not. It was just going to happen.

Victoria walked into the bedroom after a few moments with the Blackberry in her hand. 'Actually I think as you have bashed your head it may be better that I email them, otherwise they may think you are better than you really are.'

Mike just sat against the bed, his mind in turmoil. Surely she had seen the black bra? Was she not going to say anything? Was she going to play some sort of mind game, catch him out? But he knew Victoria, she would have gone mad with fury, she could not have controlled her voice and pretended nothing was wrong, surely?

'God, you really do not look good at all darling, you are as white as a sheet! I'll email them and then help you up. Would you like a coffee or do you think it would make you throw up?' Victoria was standing over him, Blackberry in hand looking concerned.

'Coffee, yep, that sounds good. Perhaps you are right I should take it easy today.' Mike just looked up at his wife, in her old T-shirt and black lacy knickers and was dumbfounded.

Victoria returned from the kitchen a few minutes later with a mug of coffee in one hand and still carrying the Blackberry in the other.

'I've sent an email to Georgina and said you fell out of bed. Sorry, I couldn't bring myself to say it was all my fault! I've said I'm taking you to the doctor's first thing as I am not letting you drive and then you're staying put quietly for the day. You can deal with anything on the laptop.' Victoria put the coffee down on the bedside table and straddled herself over his body, Mike was still sitting on the floor with his back against the bed.

Victoria placed her arms around his upper body just below his armpits and heaved him up onto the bed. Then she swung his legs onto the bed and pulled the duvet over him. Sitting up in bed he reached for the coffee, still unable to quite comprehend what was happening. Perhaps, thought Mike, his bump on the head had been more serious than he had realised, and he had not stuffed Sophie's bra in his laptop bag. In which case, where the hell had he put it?

Victoria sat on the end of the bed looking at him. 'I am

sure Georgina – it is Georgina your new secretary isn't it? – will forward anything important for you. Now, after you've come to a little with that coffee, let's get you in the shower and I'll ring the doctors. I'm serious, I really don't want you to drive before you have been checked out.'

The morning seemed to pass in a bit of a haze to Mike. He was not certain whether it was the bang on the head or the worry over Sophie's bra. He was driven by Victoria to the doctor's who, after an over-thorough examination, pronounced him fit and well.

'I'm going to open up the shop, darling.' Victoria said as she packed away the plates into the dishwasher after their ham sandwiches and cup of tea which had made up an early lunch.

'Well then I shall set myself up in the study and see how my partners have coped without me for the last few hours,' Mike responded, as he started to push himself down the corridor to the study and his laptop bag, which he had not been able to check all morning.

As Victoria left the house with a cheery goodbye Mike settled himself at his desk and reached into his bag. He withdrew the laptop and some loose papers and shuffled his hand around but there was definitely no bra. That meant only two things, either he didn't put it in there – perhaps that was a dream. In which case where the hell was it? Or Victoria had removed it and was waiting for her moment to confront him with the evidence.

Mike played with the idea in his head.

'I stand before you my Lord, as Victoria wife of Michael and exhibit in my right hand a black lacy bra size 32D.' Victoria was addressing a packed court room in Mike's mind. 'My husband claims no knowledge and I believe he is lying!'

'Now how the hell do I defend that?' thought Mike, as he relaxed back into his chair.

'You owe me, big time, you tart!' Andrea was sitting in the sunlight at a railway station platform. There were no announcements or other passengers milling about. The station seemed old fashioned, clean and small as though some type of quintessential branch line from the 1950s.

'I moved the bra for you. I got to the laptop bag before Victoria and stuffed it behind the books on gardening on the shelf in your study. I could not take it with me across the divide so to speak and I did not have that much time to act in.'

'Thank you, I don't know what to say,' Mike was relieved beyond words and also very pleased to be seeing Andrea again.

'Could I suggest you try not to get yourself into that position again? I mean you really should not go around collecting young ladies' underwear as some sort of pervert trophy thing!' Andrea had a mischievous smile and her eyes were sparkling. 'That was actually the first time I have been back into your world, although it is not really the same.'

Mike was sitting beside her on the bench. Their thighs were casually touching and he reached across to hold her hand.

'You are turning into my guardian angel, aren't you?' Mike smiled at her and squeezed her hand gently. 'I'll dispose of the item in question when I wake up, before Victoria comes home. What do you mean about the place not really being the same?'

'Oh God, Mike it is so hard to describe! You feel emotionally that walls and things are not really solid. I suppose for me back in your world is a little like you in this world when you dream. Things melt away, you move as though you are floating.' Andrea knew what she had experienced but could not find the words to help Mike understand.

'Well all I know is I am so grateful… again!' Mike was pleased at least he understood why Victoria had not found the bra. 'I like this railway station, rather quaint really. Is a steam train going to come along in a minute?' Mike asked, as he looked first one way and then the other up the platform.

'I have no idea if a train is going to come along, Mike!' Andrea smiled, she thought Mike looked like a small boy excited at the thought of going on a steam train. 'Could I suggest that you don't make this too long a visit here, you should deal with your young lady's underwear before the lovely wife comes home!'

'That's true. I tend to lose track of time here, sorry no pun intended!' Mike looked across at Andrea and smiled. 'I would like to come back here again and wait for the train. Perhaps they might have a restaurant carriage and we could have tea and cakes as the countryside rolls past.'

'That would be lovely, bye for now.' And with that Andrea stood up, started to walk up the platform and seemed to melt away. Mike woke up and started to rub his eyes as he looked out of the window of his study. He looked at his email page, 86 in his inbox since this morning.

'Surely there must be more to life than this.' He thought, 'Yes there is, it is called death and the more I think about it the more I like the sound of it.'

Mike pushed himself over to the bookcase, it was low level like all the ones in the house to accommodate his needs in his chair. He looked along the gardening section and pulled a couple of books out. There stuffed behind them was the black bra. Mike decided he should dispose of it completely so he pushed himself into the kitchen picked out the rubbish in the bin liner from under the sink and dropped the bra into it. He tied up the bag and pushed himself outside, opened and dropped it safely into the black bin. That, he thought with some satisfaction, was not going to be recycled.

Victoria came home a little after 5pm and they spent another uneventful evening followed by a rather boring weekend. The only odd conversation happened on Sunday morning when Mike had suggested they visit the steam railway at Alresford, a few miles east of Winchester.

'God, Mike has that bang on your head affected you that badly?' Victoria responded to the idea

'It is just I thought it would be different, they have a special 1940s theme and we could have a ride on the train, some tea out, just chill really.' Mike tried to sound nonchalant.

'Well unless you are starting to regress into a 7-year-old who wants to go and play on steam engines I would rather go over and see Gerald and Jules and sit and drink Pimms. You can drive.' Victoria sounded as though her mind was made up and Mike did not feel able to argue. In fact he thought it would still not be as good to visit the railway line with Victoria as it would be with Andrea, so what the hell.

The rest of the Sunday had passed in a blur, Victoria had drunk a little too much Pimms and had started to plan her next holiday with Jules while Gerald had bored Mike with details of his latest bonus deal at work that he was trying to funnel to some offshore account to avoid tax.

That evening as they got ready for bed Mike was pleased at the idea of going to sleep and dreaming of Andrea, perhaps after such a day he would be able to travel there at will again. Even if he could not then there would be work this week and he could spend most of his waking hours away from Victoria and home. She had annoyed him that afternoon more than he was prepared to admit to himself. It seemed odd but one moment she had been so supportive and attentive when he had banged his head on the table on Friday and then they had seemed to settle into their usual routine of two middle-aged people sharing a house, not exactly a happy marriage.

'Darling…' Victoria was taking off her blouse and had already removed her jeans, she was standing in front of Mike, who was sitting on the edge of the bed not really taking any notice.

'Darling...' Victoria repeated herself and Mike looked up. Her blouse was open and her breasts peeking out. 'Would you like to help me out of the rest of my clothes?'

'Not really.' Mike was still thinking about slipping off to sleep and spending time with the woman who was now occupying more of his thoughts than his wife. 'To be honest love I am really not in the mood and I thought you drank a little too much this afternoon.'

'Well, fuck you, or rather I won't!' Victoria turned her back, stalked into the en-suite and slammed the door behind her.

When she finally walked back into the bedroom Mike had already pulled the duvet over his body and had drifted off to sleep. Victoria looked down at him, her anger had not subsided.

'Well I am going off to the spare room, that's where you belong after that approach you bloody cripple.' Victoria walked down the corridor and settled comfortably into the spare bedroom bed. This was not the first time she had slept in here and as she snuggled down she thought that she actually liked it more than the master bedroom. Mike had been spending so much time with his head full of work recently that she felt rather distant from him. Did they used to share so much together, or was that just her imagination? It was like looking back to your childhood, the summer holidays always lasted for ever and were hot and sunny.

'Perhaps it is a little like that in marriage, the early years always seem so good but in fact they were not necessarily better, just hindsight with rose tinted spectacles,' Victoria thought as she rolled onto her side. The bed felt large and empty and she liked the feel of the slightly cooler side without a body in the way of her legs as she spread herself across the whole width.

CHAPTER 6

FOR THE following week Mike and Victoria subsided into what could best be described as trench warfare. While there wasn't exactly the mud of the Somme, there were other obvious similarities. After the initial cut and thrust of the battle on Sunday night, the rattle of machine gun fire of their words, there ceased to be any more blatant disagreements. Merely a comfortable distance between their respective armies. They had both dug in and were keeping their heads down. Victoria had spent most of Monday and Tuesday evening moving some of her personal belongings into the spare bedroom. In a way was this her drawing up the battle lines that they would fight over till exhaustion engulfed them say in four years' time? Was Victoria making sure her trench was secure, her lines of communication and supplies well set up? What Mike was not certain about was what action he should be taking while all this was going on. He did manage one lob of a hand grenade which was despatched by Victoria with a verbal swat that left him knowing any further action at this time would be futile.

'Darling, this is ridiculous,' he had said as she carried her fifth box of shoes into the spare bedroom on Monday. Well was that a hand grenade or an olive branch?

'You complain I get drunk with my friend, out of the blue suggest we go to a bloody steam rally and then refuse to have sex. I suggest we start a dialogue after you have finished your mid-life crisis.' And with that Victoria had turned and walked out of the bedroom leaving Mike sitting on the bed, wondering where it was all going to end.

After Pilates on Thursday evening, Victoria settled down for a heart-to-heart with Jules. 'I tell you, I have about had enough.' She started just as soon as the first large glass of white was in front of her. They were propped at the bar in their favourite wine bar in a side street in Winchester. It was virtually empty.

'Truth is Mike has been acting bloody strangely over the last few months. I have been thinking it was that bang on his head but in fact it has been going on for longer than that. What is really scary is I feel more comfortable in the spare bedroom. I can read and turn the light out when I like and sex has been such a non-event for years, I don't even miss it.' Victoria sipped her wine, it was going down a little too quickly but she did not seem to care. 'Well when I say I don't miss sex, I mean I don't miss it with Mike, I still relax on my own, and to be honest it makes that sort of thing a little easier being in the spare room.' The wine had made Victoria even more relaxed and uninhibited with Jules than normal.

'Gerald and I have not shared a bedroom for years. Although I guess it is a little easier as I know he will be away staying at his club in London at least one night a week.' Jules placed a comforting arm around her old friend. 'I think most marriages end up like this. After all why would we want to share a bed with some old git who does nothing but fart and snore?'

Both the women laughed.

'Doesn't Sophie think it a little odd though?' Victoria asked.

'I don't know and to be honest I don't really have the relationship with my daughter to ask. After she hit puberty it was just hell and we have never really got on since. She has her life at university, she seems happy enough. Gerald is always busy in the city, making the cash. I have to say I do appreciate that element of my husband, he provides very nicely and so I am prepared to ignore his indiscretions.' Jules appeared relaxed at explaining her dysfunctional family and addressed it almost matter of factly.

'I suppose we've never really talked about these things, I'd just always assumed most of what you've just said. I didn't realise you and Sophie aren't close, but it's pretty obvious over you and Gerald. I hope you don't mind me saying so?'

Victoria drained her glass and looked down the bar for the bartender. He was leaning over, chatting to a girl who was propped the other side. She was drinking while he was meant to be serving.

'God, he has got a nice bum,' Victoria said. 'Excuse me, could we have a top up please.' The bartender casually looked up, raised himself to what must have been nearly 6ft 3 inches and walked down the bar smiling at Victoria and Jules.

'Ladies, I am sorry, of course, two dry white wines. Large wasn't it?' Victoria was sure there was a twinkle in his eye as he addressed them.

After he had poured out their drinks he returned to his pose at the other end of the bar and recommenced his conversation with the girl.

'Now that would be a bit of fun for a Friday night,' said Jules as she followed Victoria's gaze back down the bar. 'Of course I don't mind you saying about Gerald. I think everyone in bloody Winchester realises how we are together. But what are we going to do about you and Mike? That is the real question?'

'God knows. I've tried ever since we found out we couldn't have kids. I have had the shop, he works, we enjoy our evenings, our meals, a glass of wine, it's all very easy if you know what I mean.' Victoria stopped looking at the barman and turned to her friend.

'Well you seem to be describing two people sharing a

house not a marriage. Perhaps you should just have a little honesty between you both.' Jules was always so self-assured with her views, thought Victoria.

'You mean lead separate lives?' Victoria asked and then found her head turning back down the bar.

'Well if you could stop looking at that boy for a minute!' Victoria was stung into action by her friend's words and turned to face her again.

'Sorry Jules, you have my attention!'

'Look, I don't know if you and Mike are drifting apart, reached the end of the road or what. All I do know is that it must have been a hell of a strain on you with him in that chair most of the time and perhaps you owe it to yourself to live a little. That may be just sleeping in the spare bedroom for a while, it may be more.' Jules lifted her glass and took a sip.

'You're right of course. Let's just see what time brings, no need for rash decisions and I do think Mike is happier with the current arrangements at home. Perhaps I have been too demanding on him physically and he would rather we had our own space.' Victoria took one last drink from her glass and it was empty.

'We need to get going,' said Jules 'You know where I am if you ever need me.'

As the two friends stood up from their bar stools they gave each other an impromptu hug.

'Thanks Jules, you're a good friend. Next week, let's get

down to planning our holiday in more detail.' Victoria said as they walked from the bar. 'I feel the need for sun, sea and well, let's just say I may not say no to anything else if the right offer came my way at the moment.' Victoria tried to look casually over her shoulder at the young bartender as they walked through the door, the action was not lost on her friend Jules.

CHAPTER 7

WHAT HAD started as trench warfare from 1916 evolved into the Cold War. There wasn't even the odd barbed comment any more, Mike was happy with being left alone in the master bedroom. He felt less self-conscious when he lurched into the en-suite for his nightly pee. Victoria seemed pleased to be able to sit up and read late into the night without disturbing him. She even treated herself to a small flat-screen TV so she could watch a film in bed, something that Mike would never have condoned. As she unwrapped it, she felt pleased with the little piece of independence that it gave her.

'Well, Michael you will not be complaining about being kept up late and then missing that sodding commuter train.' Victoria thought to herself as she looked through the instructions and placed the remote on the bedside table.

'Nice TV,' said Mike, looking around the door as he pushed

himself up the corridor on his way to bed. 'Don't you think it makes the place look like a hotel room though?'

'A hotel room is designed for comfort and so that is fine with me,' replied Victoria. 'Although I have to say a hotel room is also usually temporary accommodation, but this is permanent!'

'Sorry for asking,' Mike responded as he pushed on into the master bedroom and closed the door behind him.

After he climbed into bed he drifted off to sleep quickly. He had not dreamt of Andrea since Victoria had moved into the spare bedroom. He had tried to think of her but could not seem to link up with the alternative life.

'Well I'm pleased to see we're finally going to make some time for each other.' Andrea was laying on the grass on a picnic blanket in a pair of jeans and a loose baggy jumper.

'Where have you been? I have so wanted to see you.' Mike did not want to sound accusing but had missed her over the recent weeks.

'Well you know I have been watching how things have been unfolding with Victoria. I can sense these issues and thought there should be a little space between us. I feel responsible for what is happening in your marriage. I thought you and your good lady, if I can call her that, should have a little time to sort things out.' Andrea smiled up at Mike, he was standing, not sure whether to sit or recline beside her.

'In the end, I thought I'd given it enough time and frankly

was missing you, so here I am. Why don't you sit down and relax? I guess now you could share a glass of wine without the risk of being discovered!' Andrea tapped the rug next to her. Mike sat down, stretched out his legs and looked at the view. Andrea passed him a chilled glass of white wine, where she had got it from he was not quite sure. It had just appeared.

'Thank you. I've missed you too.' Mike sipped his glass. 'Lovely – a chilled dry white to accompany a lovely view. I really don't know how we manage to end up in places like this but I do find it relaxing. The last time we saw each other was on the old station platform. '

'I remember, you had wanted a steam train to come along.' Andrea raised her glass also containing the same chilled white wine.

'Well that was the weekend that started everything off. I had suggested a steam train ride for a change with Victoria, it seemed natural after the dream and she frankly went off on one. By Sunday night she had moved into the spare bedroom.'

'Mike, Mike be honest with yourself, it was going wrong long before that, long before we had started meeting in your dreams.' Andrea sounded supportive, not accusing. 'The truth is Mike, no one has affairs if they are happily married. While we've only hugged, we're more drawn to each other than you are with Victoria. And while we are on the subject, if I had not intervened, your dick would have been in that Sophie's mouth about as quickly as you could have got it out from your trousers. I would hardly say that was the action of a happily married man! You were tempted, let's just accept that.'

Mike stood up suddenly. He did not need to be reminded of his evening with Sophie. He dropped the glass and it fell to the ground with a smash, wine flowed across the rug and splashed up his trouser leg.

He turned over in bed and saw Victoria standing over him. His hand still held a now empty glass of water and the duvet was soaking. He could feel the dampness reaching his pyjama bottoms.

'Well that is a bloody mess. You must have dozed off holding the glass, in your sleep you sort of called out and because I am the considerate wife that I am, though God only knows why, I came in to help!' Victoria looked angry and not a little upset at the thought of extra washing.

'Thank you for coming in, I am sure I could manage though.' Mike felt rather helpless, he knew he would need his wife to change the bed whilst he sat in his chair. He could do it but it would take ten times as long and cause a lot of noise and therefore disturb her in the spare bedroom.

'Well you had better get out of bed whilst I get the new duvet and cover. Push yourself over there in the corner out of the way so I can work my way around both sides of the bed.' As Victoria left the room Mike got himself into his chair and positioned it as instructed. He watched as Victoria stripped the wet duvet off and set to work stuffing the clean one into a new cover and placing it on the bed. He watched as she bent over the duvet to straighten it. She was wearing an old white T shirt of his and no knickers.

'There was a time when I would have playfully spanked that arse at this point,' he mused to himself. Victoria still had an attractive body but somehow Mike had no urge to touch it. He had spent years touching it and he had no wish to do so again. 'Why had it gone this far?' He thought to himself.

'There,' said Victoria, as she straightened up. 'Dry bedclothes. Now I'm off to watch the rest of my film in bed. Thanks for helping me miss the start.'

She walked to the door and calmly shut it behind her. Mike pushed his chair to the side of the bed and lifted himself into a sitting position on it and then swung his legs up with both hands under his knees.

'Goodnight, and thank you!' He called, though he could tell from the volume of the television that Victoria was unlikely to hear. Mike slipped his body under the sheets and wondered if he would see Andrea again in his dreams.

CHAPTER 8

IN FACT it was not for a couple more nights, on a Friday, that Mike went to sleep and saw Andrea laying on the same picnic rug in the same meadow. Only this time she was wearing one of her wrap-around silk dresses that he loved.

'If I offer to pour a glass of wine for you are you going to try not to spill it?' She asked almost mischievously

'Promise, as long as you promise not to mention Sophie. That really hurt.' Mike reached out his hand and took the glass that Andrea was proffering.

'Well frankly you should learn to be a little less precious. I said it as I saw it. I was not meaning to be judgemental. You're a bloke and why would you not have gone for it, unless of course you were in a fulfilling loving whole relationship with someone who made you feel special all the time.' Andrea looked up from her seating position on the rug, her blonde fringe framing her piercing blue eyes as she looked up at him.

Mike started to feel aroused. He was standing up, close to her, he had taken the glass of wine but not sat down. He was staring down at her dress, the way it curved over her breasts and it fell slightly open down her cleavage. He realised that he would have to sit down as it was getting pretty obvious his groin was straining at his trousers.

Andrea smiled up at him. 'I suggest you come and sit down young man,' she said, aware of the effect she was having on him but not wanting to be too direct and cause him any embarrassment.

'That sounds like an invitation that's hard to refuse.' Mike sat down beside her, their legs casually touching. He carefully placed his glass on the rug beside him. He did not want to ruin this moment. He had not felt this turned on since Sophie. But at the same time this also felt different, more meaningful, less blatant and gratuitous.

Andrea also put down her glass and placed an arm around him. As they kissed Mike felt as though he would never feel the same again. This is what it should be like. They lay in each other's arms, the sky above was blue and there was bird song coming from trees nearby. They spent time stroking each other, gradually undressing each other, drinking in their respective bodies with their eyes. This was a moment to savour, for both of them.

After they made love, Mike held Andrea close, wanting to be one with her. They gently dozed off happy and content.

As Mike woke up he was pleased to see he was still with Andrea, he had not woken in his other life. He preferred to think of it that way as opposed to real life. This felt more real, and so his living life was simply just different.

'Darling,' it was Andrea who spoke first. 'I think I really am now the other woman. We've crossed a line – we're having an affair.'

'Well I'm inclined to agree,' said Mike. 'Although I think Victoria would find it hard to name you in divorce proceedings! I guess I would just exhibit in my defence your death certificate!'

The both laughed out loud at the ridiculous situation that they were in.

'Bye for now, we must go our separate ways.' Andrea pecked him on the cheek, stood up and walked away, melting into the distance, in the way Mike had got used to.

As the next morning was Saturday, Victoria usually started early in the house, stripping the beds and putting a wash on before opening up the shop. Mike was happy to do some chores and then brave the supermarket for the weekly shop.

As Mike was in the en-suite, he heard Victoria pull off the duvet and start the usual routines.

'Jesus, Mike, have you reverted to being a teenager?' Victoria was nothing if not direct in recent days and weeks.

'What? I'm cleaning my teeth. Whatever you are wittering on about I am sure can wait till I have had a shower?' Mike had grown accustomed to the bluntness of their communications. Victoria pushed open the door from the bedroom. She stood framed by the opening, the bed sheet in her hand.

'Mike I appreciate you're a bloke, have needs etc… but if you are going to wank in the night can you at least do so in the bathroom. This sheet is disgusting, are you 14?'

Mike looked at his wife. He had started to get used to the feeling of indifference that had been growing in him where she was concerned over the last few weeks. However, what was welling up in him now were thoughts of real loathing. What he had experienced last night with Andrea had been special beyond words and to now have Victoria somehow denigrating it was more than he could bear. Mike pushed himself towards his wife, she remained standing in the doorway.

'You miserable fucking bitch. Whatever happened in my bed, please note the term my – not our – bed is none of your sodding business, you dried-up barren old cow! I appreciate you do the washing, but when I last checked, my salary pays the mortgage, the council tax, the utilities and the bloody Tesco bill.' Victoria went to open her mouth. 'Don't you dare fucking well interrupt me. When I last checked our bank statement that ridiculous excuse for a business of yours cost us two grand the other month because you are incapable of making any money. Thank God you couldn't have children, you would have been hopeless at bringing them up too, I suggest the only work you are capable of doing is washing the sheets and if they are dirty. I don't care. Next week I'll make sure I wipe my arse on them.'

Mike had not said so much in one go to his wife in over a week.

'Now get out of my bloody way so I can get dressed. We still have to eat so I am going shopping.' Mike moved his chair towards her. Victoria just dropped the sheet and burst into tears, she ran down the corridor and into her bedroom slamming the door shut behind her. Mike could hear her sobbing but he was past caring. He had soaked up so much over the last few weeks and perhaps some of what had been said had been inside him for months, if not years.

Mike dressed himself and left the house without saying goodbye. He drove to the supermarket, got his chair out of the boot and hauled himself into it. He pushed himself from the car park and decided to go to the café first so he could have a coffee and a bacon sandwich. He was still feeling angry and the bacon sandwich, he felt, could be that little bit rebellious. After all, Victoria could not tell him off.

As he sat down and started to eat his illicit breakfast, he casually looked up and saw Sophie walking over to him.

'Oh God please not this morning. This is all I need,' he thought to himself, but he had no where to escape to so he sat and waited for her to reach him.

'Hi Mike, how are you?' Sophie said as she reached the table.

'I'm fine thanks Sophie,' Mike lied. 'Just back from uni? For the weekend?'

'Nope, Easter holidays! Back for three weeks actually. Do you think Victoria would like some help in the shop?' She sat down opposite Mike

'I don't know what my wife wants in the way of help, either in the shop or outside. Perhaps medical intervention… a frontal lobotomy may be best,' Mike replied in a dead-pan delivery, without a trace of sarcasm.

'Wow, Mike, what the fuck's wrong with you? I just asked about doing a few hours in the shop!' Sophie felt a little uncomfortable with Mike's direct approach.

'Sorry, domestic. You know, I bet your mum and dad must have them all the time… well I don't mean all the time, obviously, just some of the time…' Mike had finished his sandwich and reached for his coffee.

'Oh God yes, I know. In that sense uni has been a blessing, not having to live permanently under the same roof. Although when we last met, if you don't mind me mentioning it, you said you were happily married?' Sophie's demeanour started to change, she looked at Mike with a twinkle in her eyes. 'Or were you just trying to play hard to get?' She smirked at him.

'Shall I grab a coffee and join you?' she said, as she pushed her chair back and started to stand up.

'Sophie, I am not in a good place right now… emotionally and any conversation with you is not going to help. In fact

Victoria and I are really struggling, God alone knows if we will make it through—' Mike stopped himself and thought, 'In fact I don't even know if we want to make it through.'

Sophie leant forward across the small table and placed her arms around his neck.

'You poor thing,' she said tenderly, making sure her breasts just pushed into his chest. 'You know where I am if you ever want to chat or…' Sophie left the sentence hanging as she uncoiled herself from around him and stood up.

'I'll skip that coffee and leave you in peace.' Sophie turned and walked out of the café without a backward glance.

'Bye and thank you,' Mike called after her in an absentminded sort of a way. He was still relishing the smell of her being that close to his face and the softness of the embrace.

Mike did not undertake the usual shop that day. He had thought he would but started to adopt a different approach when he hit the fruit and veg section first with his trolley. He decided that after the morning's debacle at home he and Victoria might as well eat separately as well as sleep in different beds. If he was going to house share with his wife, then the approach that all students adopted would be the way forward, they could keep food in different cupboards and separate shelves in the fridge. Mike did think perhaps he should only buy the food for himself, but at this stage that felt like taking matters too far. So he purchased various produce he knew Victoria would eat and like and others that he would stock for personal consumption.

So for Victoria, he bought plenty of fresh cut fruit and salad, white wine, still water and yogurts, brown rolls, a number of packets of oriental soup and some boneless chicken breasts. For himself, he purchased apples and bananas, red wine and beer, sparkling water and white rolls. He treated himself to a steak for the evening, green salad leaves and avocado. He purchase cheese and ham and some extra condiments, redcurrant jelly and English mustard.

Mike found the exercise surprisingly cathartic, was this another step in moving on with his life? What stage came after the Cold War he thought to himself, would this be winning the peace, or did that come along way down the line?

When Mike got the shopping home he spent most of the rest of the day moving the contents of the kitchen cupboards around. He separated out the crockery and cutlery, labelled doors as being either Mike or Victoria and then split the food between cupboards in a similar way. For his ease he placed most of his cupboard contents on the floor units and most of Victoria's in the higher units. He split the fridge by shelf and labelled those as well.

When he'd arrived home, he'd half-expected Victoria to still be in her bedroom and he was pleased to find the house empty. She had obviously driven into Winchester to run the shop for the day he thought.

By 5.30, the work was complete and Mike felt himself in control of his own destiny. It had after all been Victoria who had moved out of the bedroom lock, stock and barrel and so why should he not return the favour and split their kitchen up?

'Time for a cold beer,' he thought to himself as he placed the last sign on the fridge door shelf that he had filled with bottles of his favourite lager.

Mike helped himself to one, opened the bottle and, holding it between his knees, pushed himself into the back garden to sit on the decking to enjoy the warmth of the sunshine. Their garden faced west and as the sun started to sink closer to the wall at the end of the lawn, Mike felt more relaxed in his real life than he had for some time. Perhaps he mused this gradual separation from Victoria was making it easier to spend quality time with Andrea.

The front door opened and Mike heard his wife's footsteps she came straight out through the sitting room garden doors and onto the deck.

'I am so glad to see you relaxed after your outburst this morning. I hope you enjoy your evening, I am going to shower and change and have an impromptu evening out with Jules. Apparently Gerald is at some weekend corporate golf do and she popped into the shop today for a chat – we arranged it then. Don't bother to get up, oh silly me, I forgot you can't!' Victoria did not even wait for his reply as she turned on her heels and walked back into the house and Mike heard the bedroom door slam shut. He drained his beer and pushed himself into the kitchen to get another.

It took Victoria around an hour and a half shuffling between the family bathroom and the spare bedroom to get ready. When she finally emerged, she did not look like Mike had seen her for a good few years. Her hair was up, full make-up with a tight cocktail dress that had a slit up one thigh and a plunging neck line. Mike had to admit his wife looked very attractive, although he realised it was not for his benefit.

'Don't wait up sweetie, heaven knows what time I'll be back,' Victoria said sarcastically as she swanned towards the front door. 'Enjoy your wank darling. You never know I may find a man capable of standing up while we snog.' And with that she was gone through the door.

CHAPTER 9

MIKE WAS surprised how the following weeks panned out. He slept in the master bedroom, commuted to work and when he returned, Victoria was sometimes there and sometimes not. He would fix his own dinner, almost without fail open a bottle of red wine and, after he had stacked the dishes in the dishwasher, would either adjourn to the study to work or the sitting room to watch sport on TV.

Victoria had started to go out more often than not. Sometimes straight from work and sometimes she would come home first and then go out, usually looking rather lovely, or so Mike thought. He had not really considered Victoria in this way for some months now (or had it been years?) but now when she went out, Mike could not help but feel a little jealous.

Despite the fact that they now seemed to be living two separate lives, Mike had been unable to make any further contact with Andrea. Their last meeting had seemed so special, so he thought, and yet he went to sleep night after night unable to connect with the woman that he loved. After two months, Mike started to doubt the relationship he had built up with her. The afterlife, the connections through his dreams, the life in death that had felt more real than his own living seemed to elude him.

Even Victoria started to notice.

'Darling,' she said in a voice heavy with sarcasm on a Saturday morning, 'I can't help but notice the sheets have been remarkably clean for the last few weeks. I do hope you have not lost the use of everything down there now. I mean for a chap of your age that really must be a problem.'

Mike could not bring himself to say anything. Perhaps she was right, in which case did it even matter? Mike knew that in his other world everything worked fine, even his legs.

That night Mike had an early night. Victoria had gone out with Jules, supposedly to try a new restaurant that had opened in Winchester, and there was nothing much on television. As Mike swung himself into bed he hoped he would see Andrea and they could walk and talk, he missed her so much.

'Mike.' Andrea was standing in front of him on a bridge over a river. It was a footbridge and there did not seem anyone else around. Below them a clear stream rushed by no doubt making its way towards the sea. The water was sparkling and bright green plants drifted in the current.

'This could be the Test Valley,' thought Mike, 'a few miles from Winchester.'

'Mike, this is really not easy for me to say.' Andrea was looking directly into his eyes, she seemed upset.

'Hang on a minute, before you get into some deep and dark personal shit, I have missed you!' Mike could not help himself as he tripped over his own words. They spilled out like he was some ineloquent teenager. 'It has been bloody weeks and I wanted to see you every night. I have gone to sleep thinking of you, but you are never there. Did the last time we meet mean nothing to you?'

Mike sounded accusingly, he regretted his tone the moment the words were out, but he tried to reconcile himself with the idea that they needed to be said.

'Mike just calm down. I needed to give us some space. This is not easy for me either you know. I am in contact with you and see you going through all the trials and tribulations but cannot help as much as I would like. I know that there are some things that you need to work out for yourself. I feel very guilty that you've separated from your wife, even though you're still living under the same roof... because you think you're in love with a dead friend.'

'Well fuck me!' Mike was seeing red. 'Think I am in love? That's bloody rich. As God is my witness, why the sodding hell do I bother?'

'If you don't calm down, I'm going and, in case you need

to be reminded, you can't follow me Mike.' Andrea was sounding quite authoritarian.

'Well we shall see about that shall we?' Mike was in no mood to be dictated to by a dead lover.

'Oh, grow up Mike! When you've done so then perhaps we shall have another conversation.' With that Andrea climbed over the bridge and jumped into the sparkling water and disappeared from site.

'You fucking bitch!'

Mike was furious and as quickly as he uttered the words he woke up. He was sweating profusely and felt uncomfortable in his sheets. He threw them off and with his usual ungainly gait made his way into the bathroom. He stood over the toilet having a pee.

How in God's name could he get this upset over Andrea? His life was in turmoil at home, he did not even particularly care about his 20-year marriage falling apart. He had wanted to spend some time with Andrea. He had wanted to hold her, to feel close to her, to be with her and yet she'd seemed so distant.

Mike staggered back into the bedroom and instead of sitting back in bed dropped into his chair. He pushed himself out of the bedroom door and towards the family bathroom. As he did so he noticed the spare bedroom door was ajar, he looked inside, and Victoria was still not home. The room was in darkness the bed pristine.

Mike opened the vanity unit below the bathroom basin, he reached for the medicine box, and quickly found what he was looking for, several boxes of sleeping tablets. Victoria had suffered from insomnia a few years previously and the doctor had prescribed these as a solution. In practice, after taking a few over a couple of weeks the matter had settled down and so the spare packets had languished at the bottom of the box.

Mike then pushed himself towards the sitting room. He reached for the bottle of scotch from the drinks trolley and placed it in his lap where the boxes of sleeping pills were resting. He then pushed himself back into his bedroom and closed the door. He placed the bottle and the boxes of pills by his bed and positioned the chair so he could lift himself onto the duvet. He felt warm and wanted to lay on top of the covers.

'Strange,' thought Mike. 'That's the last time I'll ever sit in that sodding chair.' He reached for the scotch and swigged straight from the bottle, something he had never done in his life. Even in his most rebellious years at university, he'd used a glass for wine or spirits. Somehow to drink beer from a bottle or can was acceptable etiquette in his mind. He then reached for the first box of tablets. He popped two out of the blister pack and laid them in his hand.

'Would this be difficult?' he wondered. He opened his mouth and dropped both of them onto his tongue, he swigged again from the bottle and swallowed.

'OK, that was easy...' he said to himself. 'Just another couple of hours and I can be with Andrea full time!'

He reached for the pack and popped another couple of tablets out onto his palm. Without hesitation he popped them into his mouth. He drank from the bottle again and felt a little more relaxed. Mike looked again at his wheelchair, it had been his transport to the outside world and his prison at the same time. He had been in it during every important moment in his life since his graduation. In fact that had been the last event of his life that he had walked to unaided. Since then his graduation from Law School, his first job interview, his first court appearance, his attendance at the first partners meeting in his firm, his wedding day... yes, even his wedding day had been spent in that bloody chair.

Mike took an even longer swig from his bottle, he leaned over and pushed the chair away as hard as he could. It twisted and fell on its side and as it did so Mike nearly fell out of bed. He steadied himself and sat back on his pillows, propped up on his cushions.

'Fucking thing!' he said out loud. He popped two more pills out of the blister pack and placed them on his tongue, before swigging them down with scotch.

Mike had no idea of time, he felt himself drifting, and he felt peaceful and complete.

'Mike, what the fuck have you done?' Andrea was standing in a room, it was white as though it was some type of hospital room. No one else was there, she looked concerned and angry at the same time.

'I wanted to be with you.' Mike answered without hesitation and he did not straight away take in all his surroundings. 'Has it worked? God am I really here? Is this it? I have to say it reminds me of waking up after my accident all those years ago in a hospital room to find out I could not walk properly again.'

'Mike, for God's sake what have you done?' Andrea asked again. She was still standing and then Mike realised he was sitting in his wheelchair. He went to stand up and his legs collapsed and he fell heavily to the floor.

'I don't understand, why can't I stand? I thought this was heaven? I have been here loads with you, why can't I stand and walk and everything?' Mike sounded incredulous, he felt cheated and angry.

'Mike, I warned you, why didn't you listen? It's different when you are here permanently! When you visit, you can sort of determine how you are, so if your wish is to walk, then you can. Only when you're here all the time well, depending upon how you arrive you kind of stay as you were when you left the land of the living. It is practically the only rule that I have been able to figure out since I arrived here.'

Andrea was still standing, tears were running silently down her cheeks. Her eyes still sparkled but her face seemed to lack its shine. 'Mike you will always be in that chair.'

'Nooooooooooo!' Mike was suddenly back aged 21 in a hospital room with a doctor sitting on his bed holding his hand and his parents standing beside each other crying.

CHAPTER 10

VICTORIA looked down at her husband. She had stopped crying now. This was now two days since she had found him when she had got home after the night out with Jules. The evening had been fun, they had agreed their next holiday was to be to the Amalfi coast in Italy. They had enjoyed looking at the glossy pictures of the hotels in the brochures and the wine had flowed at the new Italian restaurant.

Then everything had changed when her key had turned in the lock at 11.30 that night. Why she had walked into their master bedroom, she did not know. Why she had decided not to go straight into her room she had no idea. But somehow she had done just that, walked in and seen Mike laying against the pillow, an empty bottle of scotch in his lap and all those empty boxes of pills on the floor. From that moment her life had felt as though it had stopped as well. It was all a haze now: the call to 999, the paramedics arriving so quickly it felt as though they had been parked on the drive, the trip in the ambulance to hospital just ten minutes away... And then the wait, that night and into the following morning.

'Mrs Stapleford, I am so sorry' the doctor had said. 'Your husband has clearly taken an overdose. He is alive but in a coma.'

'What does that mean?' had been the only question she could muster, it seemed so inadequate.

'Well, he is alive but not really responding. He can breathe on his own but the tablets and the fact that his heart had stopped before the paramedics arrived may mean he has brain damage. I am so sorry, but at this stage we really cannot be specific, we simply don't know what damage has occurred. He may be fine when he wakes up.' The doctor looked a little uncomfortable.

'So when will he wake up?' Victoria felt this was all too much to take in.

'Well, I'm very sorry, but we don't know.' The doctor shifted uneasily where he was standing.

'So he may or may not wake up, he may or may not have brain damage and you actually have no idea how long all this could go on for! Well excuse me for being blunt but I can so see where my taxes go on the NHS.' Victoria burst into tears.

That had been yesterday and now she was sitting beside him, marvelling at all the tubes and machines that surrounded him. Then there was the constant coming and going of staff in different uniforms undertaking slightly different functions to keep the hospital and her husband functioning.

Victoria reached for Mike's hand on the top of the bedclothes.

Did she want him to live? She startled herself at the bluntness of the question that went through her mind.

'Lost' was the only word that came back to her. She would be lost without him.

'Mike, please can you hear me. I am so sorry. I know it has been horrid lately but I love you so much.' As she said the words out loud, she felt warm tears run down her face all over again. They splashed on their hands that were lying entwined on the covers.

'Mike, please wake up, I am lost without you, I am so sorry, please wake up.'

Victoria felt a hand gently lay itself on her shoulder. She looked up and saw an elderly chaplain standing quietly beside her.

'I am sorry, I did not mean to disturb my dear,' he said in a low smooth voice. 'Shall I pray for you and your loved one?'

'Thank you,' was all that Victoria could utter, as she felt more tears roll down her cheeks.

CHAPTER 11

'MIKE, we need to talk.' Andrea was again standing while Mike was in his wheelchair, the room was white and clinical, it was neither warm nor cold, it was non-descript in every way.

'Look, it's like this,' she went on. 'You actually have a choice, you have not really arrived here yet. You can go back if you want.'

'I don't understand,' Mike was feeling very confused. He had spent the last six months or more moving between two worlds, sometimes by design but mostly by accident. When he had finally decided which world to spend his time in, he seemed to have failed to get past customs. He had nothing to declare!

'Mike, you are in a coma. You're in hospital and Victoria is worried shitless. She has not left your bedside for four days. Mike all you have to do is open your eyes and you're back in the land of the living.' Andrea's voice was wavering with emotion.

'Mike you can't stay, you know what it will be like here now, permanently I mean. You will be in a chair and it will not be like before.' Andrea's face was streaked with tears.

'You have to go, I have to let you go. You have a chance to finish living your life.' Andrea broke down and sobbed.

'Can I still—'

'No, Mike, this is the end, here and now. I will not be in your dreams any more. You have had a chance of seeing what it's like in this world – that in itself is a real privilege. Use it to live your life to the full.' Andrea did not try and hide her emotion.

'Well, what if I want to stay?' Mike was feeling belligerent. He had taken the tablets and the scotch. If he wanted to die, he could make that decision. Who had the right to deny his wishes?

'Mike, you don't choose like that. If you stay, you do so with all your inabilities of life. It is not your time now, don't you see? You are being punished for coming here too early. You want this life to be perfect but if you arrive when you're not called you don't get the heaven you want.'

'You mean God is punishing me? Just when I was getting my head around all this, you throw religion at me!' Mike's voice sounded incredulous.

'God, Allah, whatever, the name is irrelevant. The idea is

a higher source, person, energy, an accumulation of all of us in an entity that is good, whatever it is, whatever you believe. Just understand, if you have the chance to live, then start fighting for it. Fight for Victoria, in case you've forgotten she's your wife. She's falling apart because you're not in her world.'

Andrea looked down at Mike, her shoulders shaking with emotion as she continued to sob through her words.

'Mike, we were lucky, we had something amazing, and I came back for you because I wanted to connect with you. If I had not done so, then you would not be in this place. Right at the start, do you remember I said you weren't given a manual here? Well I bloody well wish you were, because I reckon I have broken every rule there is! I don't regret it, but now I have a chance to put it right.'

'Please can I have a hug?' Mike looked up from his chair at Andrea.

'Yes, my darling, of course.' She bent down and wrapped her arms around his neck and buried her wet, tear-drenched cheek against his. 'Goodbye, sweetheart…'

And Andrea melted away.

'Nurse! Nurse! For fuck's sake come here, he just opened his eyes! Nurse! Nurse! Get someone quickly, nurse!' Victoria was standing by the bed, Mike's hand still in hers. She was looking wildly round the small room, shouting, tears running down her face.

'Nurse! For Christ's sake, someone! My husband just opened his eyes!'

EPILOGUE

MIKE was sitting in his wheelchair looking at a windswept airport. The rain lashed against the window. It was January and although the airport lounge was warm, Mike felt a chill run down his back as he looked at the outside.

'Darling,' Victoria wandered across carrying two coffees and a large Danish pastry on a tray. 'I know you said you didn't want anything but well, I thought this may tempt you,' she said as she bent to place the tray on the table in front of him.

'Do you mind if I go down to that shoe shop on the lower level and try on a couple of pairs? They still have their new year sale on.' Victoria smiled at him.

'Of course I don't mind, silly! I'll stay here, I think the escalator could be a bit tricky!' Mike smiled back at his wife. He felt contentment, something that had been growing inside him now for months since that fateful time last autumn. He watched her stroll casually across the lounge and down the escalator. Her hair had grown and flowed down her back, it was longer now than it had been for a few years.

He gazed out of the window. He had not dreamt of Andrea since he had woken up in hospital. He still thought about her, but even that was becoming less frequent.

'She seemed so much more relaxed,' he thought to himself as he turned from the window and back to where Victoria had disappeared down the escalator.

After he had been released from hospital, they had spent a long time talking, crying and then holding each other. They had been through the pain of the accusations, particularly over what had happened with Sophie. Mike had decided to spare her some of the detail, it was unnecessary and how would he have explained the black bra? So his version of events had been true, if not the whole story.

In fact they had spoken about his obsession with work and he had told of his fears of being in his chair for the rest of his life, the separation that he felt it caused between them. At no point did Mike volunteer or Victoria question anything about Andrea. Certainly not in an intimate way. He had spoken of the way he missed his dead friend and how her sudden absence had made him think more deeply about his disability and the wish to walk freely once more. None of that had been a lie, the result of the thought process had been the same, but perhaps the route had been slightly more circuitous.

Mike would have struggled to explain his relationship with

Andrea over the last few months, and perhaps in an odd way the guardian angel that she was, she had ended up bringing him and Victoria closer together. Had he loved Andrea or in fact just the life without his wheelchair he enjoyed whilst visiting her?

'Yes, I find her very attractive,' Mike had said over Sophie. 'She is very sexy, and in fact she has offered it to me on a plate… well with a price tag attached!' Victoria had been shocked at first when Mike had explained and then decided it was rather funny.

'Rather awkward then sweetheart!' she had said with a smile. 'I don't know if I want to employ her in my shop over Christmas, or perhaps I should and overpay her to keep my husband on the straight and narrow!'

That had been the start of the discussion over Victoria's Flowers. Did it provide the right interest for her, was it a profitable business, could it be expanded in the long term? Could Victoria see herself as a florist for the next decade or more?

The end of the year had then turned into a succession of deadlines to be met as they reorganised their old lives and prepared mentally and physically for their new ones. The flower business had been put up for sale and had found an unexpected buyer virtually the moment the news had got around Winchester.

Jules had finally had enough of being a lady of leisure and

Gerald had decided to make its purchase and the gift of their house as his divorce present to his wife.

'Darling you cannot imagine how happy this makes me!' had been Jules's comment as they agreed the broad terms of the sale of the business in their kitchen on a Saturday night.

'Gerald will pay just so he can go off and start his new life with Francine. God knows what will happen when she wants a family, I mean she is nearly twenty years his junior. It's ridiculous!'

The business transaction had proceeded reasonably smoothly and by the first week in December, Victoria was working for Jules as part of the handover. The only awkward moment had been when Sophie had floated in to the shop, back from university and offering to help her mum out in the new operation.

'Vicky, love, make me a coffee please!' She had looked at Victoria with an air of superiority, which even her mother found a little hard to accept.

'Sophie, you can go and make your own coffee,' said Jules sharply. 'Victoria is here as my friend to help me understand and to get to grips with this business. She is not to be your slave.'

Jules felt a need to exert some influence over her daughter who seemed to be getting more and more unruly while at university. The divorce had not been unexpected to Sophie but the by-product had been even less contact and less influence from her father.

'Thanks, Jules.' Victoria acknowledged her friend. She also took considerable delight later in the afternoon to find herself alone in the shop with Sophie when Jules was out delivering orders.

'Sophie, you should know, Mike and I have spent many weeks talking and reconnecting. We may have struggled and this year has been difficult, but we are now closer than we have ever been. I can also tell you that he has told me everything. It has been painful at times, but we are now stronger than before. So just in case you are wondering, he will not be getting his cheque book out just so he can stick his dick down your throat… dear!'

Victoria turned and walked out of the shop. She felt brilliant and smiled broadly as she thought about telling Mike about her chat with Sophie that evening.

Christmas had been quiet as they had packed up the house, and Mike had agreed the last files to be handed over to his work colleagues. They had been hugely supportive of his proposed sabbatical.

'Take the year, Mike, if you need it,' had been the line from his managing partner when he had chatted it through over lunch at the end of October.

'It has been a shitty year for you and Victoria and what you are proposing is bloody brave. You probably have about a year's worth of weeks owed to you in back holiday anyway.'

And so here he was, mid-January and waiting in the airport lounge for his wife who was shoe shopping downstairs. He sipped his coffee and bit into his Danish pastry as rain continued to hammer at the window.

'OK, you will have to shoot me!' Victoria was standing in front of him. 'I brought three pairs but they were such a good offer.'

'That is fine, although you can thank me later personally if you feel racked with guilt!' Mike looked up at his wife and grinned.

'Sounds like you have a deal! Has the flight been called yet?' Victoria turned around to glance at the TV screen as she sipped her coffee.

'Not yet, I see. Come on Atlanta, I want to get on the plane and get going.' Victoria sounded anxious, impatient to start their new adventure together.

'Patience poppet, we will get there when we get there... Atlanta, you are going to change my life!' Mike shifted in his chair. 'I cannot wait to dump this bloody thing and walk down those steps from the aircraft in June.' Mike patted the side of his wheelchair.

'I am so proud of you, this is so brave.' Victoria bent down and kissed him gently on the lips.

As Victoria pushed his wheelchair towards the departure gate when they were called forward for boarding, Mike looked out of the window at the waiting plane, was that a whisper in his ear?

'God speed, Michael. I still watch over you, it will all be fine. Good luck!'

Also from Splendid Books...

The definitive history of Only Fools and Horses
- Sir David Jason

Only Fools and Horses - The Official Inside Story
By Steve Clark
Foreword by Theo Paphitis

This book takes us behind the scenes to reveal the secrets of the hit show and is fully authorised by the family of its writer John Sullivan.

This engaging tribute contains interviews with the show's stars and members of the production team, together with rarely seen pictures.

Written by bestselling author Steve Clark, the only writer on set for the filming of *Only Fools and Horses, The Green Green Grass* and *Rock & Chips*, this book gives a fascinating and unique insight into this legendary series.
£9.99 (paperback)

The Official Only Fools and Horses Quiz Book
Compiled by Dan Sullivan and Jim Sullivan,
Foreword by John Sullivan

Now you can test your knowledge of the legendary sitcom in *The Official Only Fools and Horses Quiz Book*, which is packed with more than 1,000 brain-teasers about the show.

Plus there's an episode guide and an exclusive foreword by the show's creator and writer John Sullivan, who reveals some of the mystery behind the much-loved series and just how he came up with some of television's most memorable moments.
£7.99 (paperback)

The Wit and Wisdom of Only Fools and Horses
Compiled by Dan Sullivan
Foreword by Sir David Jason

The 'crème de la menthe' of the hilarious one-liners from John Sullivan's *Only Fools and Horses* have been brought together for the first time in *The Wit & Wisdom of Only Fools and Horses.*

All of Del, Rodney, Grandad, Uncle Albert, Boycie, Trigger and the rest of the gang's funniest and most memorable lines are here, making this triffic book a pukka 42-carat gold-plated bargain.
£4.99 (paperback)

The British Television Location Guide
By Steve Clark and Shoba Vazirani

This beautifully illustrated book reveals the settings for dozens of top television shows. From *Downton Abbey* to *Doc Martin* and from *Midsomer Murders* to *Broadchurch*, the book gives details of how you can visit the places you have seen so many times on television. It includes details of the locations for more than 100 television series.
£9.99 (full colour paperback)

Catching Bullets: Memoirs of a Bond Fan
By Mark O'Connell, Prelude by Barbara Broccoli, Foreword by Mark Gatiss and Afterword by Maud Adams

When Jimmy O'Connell took a job as chauffeur for 007 producers Eon Productions, it would not just be Cubby Broccoli, Roger Moore and Sean Connery he would drive to James Bond. His grandson Mark swiftly hitches a metaphorical ride on a humorous journey of filmic discovery where Bond movies fire like bespoke bullets at a Reagan-era Catholic childhood marked with divorce, a closet gay adolescence sound-tracked by John Barry and an adult life as a comedy writer still inspired by that Broccoli movie magic.
£7.99 (paperback)

Postcards From A Rock & Roll Tour
By Gordy Marshall, Foreword by Graeme Edge

Postcards From a Rock & Roll Tour is drummer Gordy Marshall's witty and wry take on life on the road touring with legendary rock band *The Moody Blues.*

Part memoir, part travelogue, it's a candid, unexpected and often hilarious account of just what it's like to travel around the world playing to sell-out audiences, living out of a suitcase and spending days and days on a tour bus.

If you thought being in a rock band was all sex, drugs and rock and roll, then think again....
£7.99 (paperback)